Howard Gurney was born in Sydney, Australia and is the author of six novels and multiple peer-reviewed medical journal articles. He works as a medical oncologist at Westmead Hospital in Sydney and is also a professor of medicine at Macquarie University, where he undertakes clinical trials for cancer patients. His first fantasy fiction novel, *Twin*, was published in 2015.

He lives in Sydney with his wife and their five children. He has also worked in Manchester, UK and travels extensively.

Other books by Howard Gurney

Path to Chaos series (fantasy)
Twin
The Thread Frays
Chaos

Dr Christopher Walker Murder Mystery series
Murder on the Ward
Death in a Chapel
Murder at The Rocks

MURDER AT THE ROCKS

A Dr Christopher Walker Murder Mystery
Book 3

Howard Gurney

This is a work of fiction and the characters are imaginary.

Copyright © Howard Gurney 2021

ISBN 978-0-6487177-2-0

Print edition 2021

CHAPTER ONE

THE AIR WAS thick like sludge, too heavy to breathe. Stale. Old and used up.

He opened his eyes. Darkness. He rolled his head. A long slit of light said it was day outside. But in this room, it was black.

It was *the* Black.

Darker than night and deeper than the earth's core. As black as his soul.

And as hot as hell.

Maybe it *was* hell?

Christopher Walker let his eyelids cut out the light. He didn't care if it was hell. Hell on earth or the real hell, what was the difference? Nothing, according to the reverend from up the road, except real hell lasted an eternity.

An eternity?

Walker opened his eyes a crack. How long had he been here? Days? Weeks? He didn't know. Didn't care. He was alive as far as he could tell so he hadn't died from dehydration. Not weeks then. But more than a few days.

He could sense the viscous air again, flowing over his trachea like treacle, in and out, in and out. His mouth and lips were dry and his tongue stuck to the roof of his mouth. Now he could feel it swelling, swelling, blocking his throat.

He sat up abruptly on his bed and tried to tear off his T-shirt but all he got was bare skin, slick with sweat. He rubbed his hand down his belly to his legs. Naked.

He jerked to his feet and stumbled towards the curtains, pulling them aside. Bright sunlight bit his eyes, dazzling him like an angel. He held his hands over his face and squinted through the glass of the French doors. No, no angel here. This was hell. There are no angels in hell.

He jerked the handle, threw the door open and stepped out onto the balcony. It was hot there too but at least the air was fresh. A gentle breeze played with the leaves of the jacaranda but brought no relief from the heat.

Walker shuffled to the edge and looked down on the street, swaying on weak legs. The sun was just above the houses beyond and a couple were walking their dog on the other side of the street, making towards the church. Bells tolled.

Just before nine then. Sunday. Or maybe Friday. The bellringers practised on Fridays.

The woman glanced up at him then jerked her head away. Her companion looked back over his shoulder and frowned at him but they kept walking.

Walker tried to cover himself but he felt dizzy and had to hang on to the balustrade with both hands. Somehow, he got inside and slumped into his chair.

Flea's chair!

He slipped forward onto his knees and then to his side and curled up on the floorboards, wrapping his arms around his head, pulling it hard into his chest. An animal moan filled his throat and lungs, wanting to escape his filthy soul. He opened his mouth to let it go free but the wail kept coming, on and on, deep from his core until, finally, it ended as a pitiful sob. He knew it would come again. He would never be free of it.

Flea!

Could it be true!?

The image of Barry Darling filled his mind – accusing, seething with rage. *'You let those beasts desecrate Felicity's body. They cooked her. You ate her!'*

Walker welcomed Darling's fury. Somehow it had kept him alive, as if the energy of that enormous hatred and anger had infused his body like electricity and refused to let him slip away.

But had he? Eaten her flesh?

He couldn't remember doing it. But they could've fed him her flesh without him knowing. He'd been delirious in a hut on the outer edge of nowhere in the New Guinea Highlands. They could've fed him anything.

And Darling said he'd found Flea's bones. Holes in her skull.

But how could he be so sure?

Walker rolled onto his back and stared at the ceiling. There was a ceiling rose with an ornate light in the centre and in one corner, the paint was cracked and mouldy. There must be a leak in the roof.

He remembered the feeling of dread he had in that hut when he started to come to. He'd tried to tell himself it was because they'd said his wife had drowned.

But there was always something else. Some *thing* that sat just on the edge of memory. Something they had done. The old woman or someone else. If only he could remember …

He closed his eyes. He didn't want to remember.

Because maybe Darling was right.

Walker stumbled down the stairs, holding tight to the handrail. His legs were weak and the clumsiness of his hand, which had started a few weeks ago, was still there. At least the double vision was gone. How long had he been in bed? He felt like one of his patients trying to get back on his feet after major surgery.

He reached the kitchen and opened the fridge door. A bottle of milk smelled off and in the vegetable crisper was a stick of wilted celery and a stump of a carrot. It didn't matter – he wasn't hungry. He went to the sink and stuck his mouth under the faucet and drank. Blimey, he was thirsty!

He wiped his mouth with the back of his hand. In the corner, he saw a movement and he squinted his eyes to focus. It was Archie, the Siberian cat from next door. He looked weak, barely raising his ginger head. He let out a quiet meow.

'Archie, what's wrong, old man? You look terrible.' He looked around the kitchen. It was dark since the curtains were drawn. He turned back to the cat. 'How long have you been here?'

Walker had a dim memory of the cat jumping through the door when he'd opened it one night. The moon had been full and Walker had been disturbed by it. He remembered it was the reason for pulling the curtains shut. It was the same moon that had looked down on him the night before Flea had drowned.

Walker screwed his eyes shut, trying to remember. They had travelled at night for some reason. Yes! They were being chased. Something about the other fellow. Walker pushed his fingers into his temples. The other fellow was an Australian. A geologist. Something had happened to him. Something bad. And the others were now chasing them. There was danger.

He shook his head. The memories refused to come back. He'd been semiconscious for over a month after he'd been washed away in the flood that had drowned Flea. And their guide. What was his name? He'd drowned too. The guide was the old woman's husband, the woman who had cared for him. Maybe it was *his* bones, not Flea's?

Archie let out another pathetic mew. His normally fluffy fur, which made him look like a little lion, was matted and flat.

'You're thirsty, aren't you, Archie? How long have we been here?'

Walker found a bowl and filled it with water and placed it next to the cat. Archie sniffed it then began to lick without getting up. Walker watched him for a while.

'Janet is going to be angry with me. She must be beside herself wondering where you are. Probably thinks you've been knocked over or something.' Walker frowned. Why hadn't she tried to find her cat? Dimly, he recalled thumps and muffled calls, coming and going, as if they had come to him in a dream.

Archie got to his feet and meowed, this time stronger. Walker picked him up and cradled him like a baby. He didn't feel as warm as usual.

'Come on, let's get you home.' He moved towards the front door then realised he was still naked. 'Whoops! Janet won't appreciate that.' He made for the stairs, still cradling the cat. 'Come on upstairs, Archie, while I get some clothes on.'

'Archie!' cried Janet after she opened the door to Walker's knock. She was an older lady with voluminous frizzy hair, a loud purple dress cut low at the front, and a myriad of bangles covering both forearms. 'Where have you been? Where did you find him, Kit? I've been worried sick.' She looked Walker up and down. 'And what's wrong with you? You look terrible. I've been knocking on your door for days.' She examined him closely. 'And still in your dressing gown.' She grabbed Archie out of his arms. 'Please don't tell me he's been with you all this time? It's almost a week.'

'Sorry, Janet.' Walker rubbed his hands through his hair. 'I've not been well. Been in bed. Didn't know he was there.'

'Didn't know? But he couldn't have got in without you letting him.'

He shrugged his shoulders. 'Sorry, I'm not myself. I didn't notice him.'

'I bashed on your door so many times. And I'm not the only one. Your old friend – what do you call him? Wendy. He was around with some other coppers a few times. And a skinny Chinese girl. I've seen her at your place before. And that other girl, the blonde – she was sniffing around as well. How many girlfriends do you have?'

Walker stood swaying on the steps. He'd expected Barry Darling to come snooping around. But Angela? He thought she'd never speak to him again. His heart sank when he thought about the blonde – Cassandra Hollow. What was he going to do with her? As far as she was concerned, they were an item.

'And another fellow,' continued Janet. 'Looked like a businessman or something. Had a briefcase. Why didn't you answer?'

Walker briefly wondered who the last person was. Probably a Jehovah's Witness. They'd been around lately. He let out a breath. 'As I said, I was sick. I didn't hear.'

'Sick! Sounds like you were near death!' She hugged the cat and gave him a kiss. Archie reciprocated by pushing his nose against hers. 'Come inside, my darling, and I'll give you some food. You must be starving.' She moved inside her door but before she closed it, she turned back. 'And there was that other bloke. Said he was a friend of yours. Looks like a Leb. Big, with tattoos all over. Like a bikie. Leather jacket with a skull on the back.'

Walker stiffened. A Lebanese bikie! What did that fellow want from him? He'd followed him to the Captain Cook Hotel when he'd meet Barry Darling before they had searched the *Sintak-5* and he also saw him the day he and Angela went to the Epping Pub. 'Don't know anyone like that. Are you sure he was after me?'

'Sure.' Janet stroked her cat. 'Dr Chris Walker, he said.'

Walker quickly surveyed the street. 'What did he want?'

'Search me. Said he had to give you something.'

Walker shook his head. 'Don't know him. But if he comes back, let me know. But don't tell him you've seen me.'

'Sure, but I'm not opening my door to him if he comes back. Mean lookin' bugger.' She kissed Archie again as she turned away and closed the door with her foot. 'Come on, my beautiful darling. Let's find you something nice to eat.'

CHAPTER TWO

'SYDNEY HOUSE PRICES are just plain ridiculous,' said Senior Sergeant Detective Barry Darling, leaning back in a desk chair in the open office area of the Parramatta Police Station that Monday afternoon. He was scrutinising the pages of the latest *Realtor* magazine, searching for a bargain, or at least something he could afford. He wasn't asking for much, just a reasonably priced terrace in Glebe or maybe even Annandale. Glebe was not the most salubrious suburb in Sydney so he figured the odds were in his favour of finding a two-bedder in his price range. But it was proving harder than he'd expected.

'Do you know, Jones, it says here that the average house price has gone up in Sydney by twenty percent in the last two years? The average house price in 1988 was one hundred and forty thousand and now, only three years later, it's over a hundred and ninety! How is anyone supposed to afford that? At this rate, I'll be living in bloody Penrith.'

'That wouldn't be so bad,' said the young constable distractedly. David Jones was well over six foot tall and fresh-faced, and was hunched over his desk, typing a report with the index finger of each hand.

'What would you know?' scoffed Darling. 'You grew up with a silver spoon in your mouth. Where was it? Hunters Hill?'

Jones grimaced uncomfortably without looking up. 'I live with my parents. But I used to play rugby out at Penrith. Looks nice. Close to the mountains.'

Darling flicked to another page. After a few moments he said, 'Whatever happened to that spunky constable from head office? Thelma Bianca. Did you ever ask her out?'

Now Jones stopped and half-turned to his boss, his face full of trepidation. 'Going out tonight, in fact. Taking her for a drink at the Hunters Hill Pub.'

Darling thought it sounded as if the youngster was asking for his approval. He looked frightened rather than excited at the prospect and Darling began to feel sorry for him. He didn't seem to have a clue.

'Good choice,' said Darling, although it was the last place he would've taken a date – mostly families and stuck-up private school girls, from memory. 'Have a steak and a few beers. You never know where it'll lead.' But Darling's words only seemed to make Jones more nervous. 'She's a nice girl,' he added. 'You two have a lot in common. Just get to know each other. No pressure.'

Now Jones smiled. 'She *is* nice and we do seem to get along.' He began typing again. 'I agree. We can just talk and get to know each other.'

'That's the spirit,' said Darling, although he didn't like the young constable's chances. He looked down at his real-estate magazine again. 'Here's one. Bridge Street, two-bedroom terrace with bathroom. One hundred and ninety-five.'

'I thought you said you can't afford that.'

'I wasn't talking about me, Jones,' he said, without raising his head. 'I was thinking about people like you.' Darling pursed his lips and circled the ad with his pen. 'Maybe *I* can. Just. I think I'll take a look this weekend.'

The possibility of buying a house made him think of Sally Biggs. He'd been on a few dates with the nurse and she'd hinted on more than one occasion that she would pay to rent a room. But he also had the feeling that she wanted more. He liked her but he didn't think he wanted that sort of a relationship right now. He wondered what she saw in him? He raised his head from the magazine and studied his reflection in the window. People thought he was of

Mediterranean extraction but, being an orphan, he couldn't say. At least he reckoned he was a snappy dresser – grey sports jacket with a black shirt open at the top and a heavy gold neck chain. No wonder Sally liked him. With a sudden surge of enthusiasm, he decided he'd ask her to inspect a house with him.

Later that evening, Darling thought he should drive past Chris Walker's place on his way home. His former friend had been missing ever since the episode at the Gap, when Craig Blinkton had died. It was now clear that Blinkton and his associates had perpetrated the three murders at Western Meadows Hospital but the circumstances around Blinkton's death were still not as clear. Angela Chee, the oncologist-in-training from the hospital, had been abducted by Blinkton, and Darling and Walker had given chase in a helicopter. The chase had ended at The Gap, a notorious cliff-face on the coast of Sydney associated with a long history of suicides. Walker and he had got split up and when Darling finally found him again, Walker had saved Angela, and Blinkton was dead after a fall from the cliff-top.

The question was – had Blinkton jumped of his own accord or had he slipped in the struggle to save Angela?

Or had he been pushed?

Even after interviewing Angela, he was no wiser.

Then Walker had disappeared. He hadn't turned up for work at the hospital and he didn't appear to be at home. Darling and other police officers had gone to his house on numerous occasions over the last week with no luck. He'd applied for a warrant to enter his premises and it had been approved that afternoon.

Darling eased his Commodore to a walking pace as he turned the corner into Lower Fort Street and the V8 engine grumbled as he coasted along in the muted light of evening. He passed Walker's house and was gratified to see a light on in the upstairs bedroom. 'Got you!'

He turned into Trinity Avenue, a short cul-de-sac opposite Walker's place, and parked outside Darling House, a grand Edwardian building now used as a nursing home. It was also his namesake. As an orphan, Darling had been left on the steps of the building and the nurses had named him after it.

This time, Walker answered his knock. The door cracked open to show Walker's face in the reflected light from the street.

'You look terrible, Kit. Where've you been? What've you done to yourself?'

Walker's face was pale and thin, his hair was in disarray and his lips split. He stared blankly at Darling for some moments, as if he didn't know him. When he opened the door further, Darling could see he was only wearing a dressing gown. Saying nothing, Walker turned away from the door but left it open and Darling followed into the dark, sparsely furnished sitting room.

He could understand his condition. The last time he had seen Walker, just after Blinkton had died, he had accused him of eating his dead wife's remains. He deserved to be like this.

'Are you going to tell me what happened?'

Walker slumped down on the lounge chair and stared numbly ahead, as if Darling wasn't there.

Finally he spoke, although he sounded as if he was in a trance. 'You seem to have worked it all out. What do you need me for?'

Darling realised he was talking about Felicity, not Craig Blinkton. He thought carefully before he spoke again. 'I found the bones, you know. Buried in the burnout fireplace in the hut.'

There was no reaction from Walker.

'The Mount Hagen police sent them on to Port Moresby. The dental records confirm that one set of bones belong to Felicity.'

Walker continued to stare blankly ahead and Darling noticed tears forming in his eyes. Soon they were streaming down his face. His immediate impulse was to comfort his old friend but he stopped himself. Whatever Walker said now could be incriminating. He had to keep focused.

Walker raised his hands to cover his eyes and sat for some moments, his body shaking. An occasional sob escaped. But then, as quickly as it had started, he became quiet and still again – blank-faced, eyes staring although still moist with tears.

'Kit, you survived in that hut for over a month. There was no food. How did you live?'

"I don't know.' His voice was flat. 'I was unconscious. Delirious. I don't even remember the hut clearly. My first clear memory is the hospital in Mount Hagen.'

'An old lady cared for you in the hut. The guide's wife.'

'I don't remember her.'

'You must remember something.'

'Just dreams and fragments. Nothing makes sense.' He paused. 'I had a feeling something bad had happened.' Now he looked at Darling. 'But I can't remember what.'

'Kit, you must tell me the truth. Did you eat Felicity's flesh? Or the flesh of the guide?'

Walker closed his eyes. His head swayed as if he was trying to remember. Finally, he looked at Darling again. 'I can't remember, Wendy. Believe me, if I had I would tell you, regardless of the consequences. I can't live with these nightmares. I want the Black to go.' He put his face into his hands and broke into sobs again.

Darling watched on, feeling helpless. He realised he should have brought another officer with him but he had not intended to push Walker about Felicity. He'd just wanted to see whether he was at home.

Eventually, Walker stopped crying and lay down on the lounge. He seemed to be going to sleep. Darling hesitated. Could he just leave? Should he leave him alone? What if he tried to hurt himself? But he reasoned that Walker had been struggling with these feeling for years so it was unlikely. If he slunk out, he'd just be heartless, not failing in his duty of care. He looked at Walker's pathetic face. Whatever he did or didn't do or know, his actions had led to the death of Felicity. He deserved the grief.

I can wear heartless, thought Darling.

'I'll leave you now, Kit,' he said. 'But I'll be back tomorrow. I need to ask some more questions.'

As he left, there was still no reaction from Walker.

CHAPTER THREE

DARLING AND JONES met at Walker's house late the next afternoon. There was no answer to their knock, despite Jones thumping heavily on the door. The neighbour – a woman with wild hair – came out to see what the noise was about and Jones reassured her and sent her back inside.

'Do you think he's topped himself, sir?' asked Jones after her door had closed.

'Hope not. Let's check the Hero.'

A quick search of the pub on the corner found that Walker was not there either so they returned to the house.

'Only one way to find out, Jones,' said Darling, pointing at the door.

Jones removed his hat, took a few steps back and launched himself at the door. The lock was flimsy and burst open with the first assault. Darling stuck his head through.

'Kit,' he yelled. 'It's me, Wendy.'

They separated and quickly searched the house, Darling on the bottom floor and Jones taking the top. Darling waited at the bottom of the stairs and Jones trudged down. 'Nothing up there, sir.'

'Let's check the Captain Cook and the Lord Nelson,' said Darling. As they left, the managed to close the front door. The cheap night latch had cracked but the original door lock still worked.

Thirty minutes later, after a fruitless search, they stood on a corner of Argyle Street. 'Looks like he's scarpered, sir,' said Jones.

'I suppose so. Where would he go, though? He's got no relatives.'

'Should I put out a missing person alert?'

Darling thought for a moment. 'Let's leave it another day. See if he turns up.'

They walked back to their cars and Jones drove off as the street lights were coming on. Darling had parked in front of Darling House. He sat in the car, thinking about his early life there. The nurses had cared for him, although he had spent a lot of his later years at Kit's place. Walker's dad hadn't minded him sleeping over. He and Kit had knocked around after school with Felicity who lived up the road with her druggy parents. Sometimes they'd go down to the docks to listen to the wharfies, other times they'd hang around the pubs hoping there'd be a fight. When they were really bored, they'd break into houses up on Kent Street and nick a few things. They didn't need the money, it was mostly for excitement. Then one day, he and Kit were caught stealing a car from an old geezer who lived at the end of Windmill Street, a clapped-out FJ Holden that was ready for the junk heap. Sergeant Bowles could have sent them to juvenile detention but instead, he gave them one last chance.

Darling let out a pent-up breath. That was all a long time ago and a lot had happened since. He glanced back at Walker's place and noticed the front bedroom light was on.

'Huh! Son of a gun.'

As he got out of his car, his attention was captured by a swarthy looking fellow sauntering along the street outside Walker's house. He hesitated at the gate, then disappeared down the next street, which had access to the lane behind the houses. As he walked away, Darling noticed he was wearing a leather jacket with a skull design on the back.

He gave a quiet whistle. 'What's a bikie want with Dr Chris Walker?'

Walker answered the knock at the door. He looked better than he did the day before but he was still wearing nothing but a dressing gown.

'Where you been?' Darling asked. 'We've been looking all over for you.'

'I was at the pub.'

'No you weren't, we checked them.'

'The Mercantile?'

Darling didn't answer.

'So, I guess it was you who ruined my front door,' said Walker.

'Don't worry, the service will pay for it.' Darling followed him into the lounge room. 'We were worried you'd hurt yourself.'

Walker grunted and looked back over his shoulder. 'If I was going to do that, I think I would have done it a long time ago.' He sat on the lounge. 'What do you want? Going to grill me again about New Guinea?'

'Not that. I've got to ask you about Craig Blinkton,' said Darling. 'I've managed to hold Head Office off for the moment but they want me to wrap it up.' He decided to be more direct. 'And I want to tell them it wasn't murder.'

Walker sat in silence for a moment then asked, 'Have you seen Angela? What did she say?'

'She says he fell.' Darling studied Walker's face carefully as he spoke. 'Says Blinkton was going to push her over the cliff but you turned up and jumped him. Says that Blinkton slipped and fell.'

Walker's head lolled back onto the chair. 'So, what are you asking me for?'

'Doesn't add up. She says you jumped at him but didn't touch him. Blinkton's pistol was missing a bullet and I heard a shot.'

'So?'

'So, tell me this – how did Blinkton miss his shot without anyone touching him? And how did he slip?'

Walker closed his eyes. He slipped his hands into the pockets of his gown and frowned as he drew something out. He held it up and studied it, then, still frowning, thrust it back into the pocket. From where Darling was standing, it looked like a silver amulet of some sort.

Walker spoke again. 'Does it matter? He was going to kill Angela. But he didn't. Why do you have to know every detail?'

Darling waited a few moments before he spoke. 'Did you push him, Kit? Did you push him to save Angela?'

Walker kept his eyes closed. 'What if I did?'

'I can see how it could've happened. Blinkton pointing a gun at Angela. You slamming into him to spoil his shot. The shot missing. Him falling off the cliff.' Darling paused. 'Is that how it happened?'

Walker sat forward on the seat. 'No, Wendy. It was just like Angela said. I jumped at Blinkton who was pointing a gun at Angela. It surprised him. He turned and pulled the trigger and missed his shot. Then he stumbled backwards over the edge. He fell off the cliff by himself.'

Darling pursed his lips. 'Okay, so that's how it's going to be. I'm trying to help you here, Kit, but if you're not going to be open with me then you're on your own. Someone from head office might start investigating. Where will you be then?'

Walker let out a laugh. 'Who? That deadshit Royce? Or his sidekick? The little blonde chick? Come off it, Wendy. You're the best of a bad lot. Don't try and scare me with a bunch of useless wankers.'

Darling was mildly surprised that Walker put him on the top of the pile, at least. Feeling suddenly generous, he thought he would impart some intel and see its effect. 'And another thing, why do you have a bikie hanging around your house? Are you branching out from murder to narcotics?'

Walker sat up straight in his chair and glanced out the front window and Darling followed his gaze. It was night but nothing showed in the dull streetlight, not even a passing car. Walker turned back to him. 'A bikie? Are you sure?'

'I saw him casing your house before I came in. He went around the back. Probably looking to break in, as we speak.'

Darling was quite satisfied with the effect his words. Walker stood and moved stealthily towards the hallway.

'Do you have your gun?' he said.

'Maybe. But what's it got to do with me?'

'You're a copper,' he growled. 'I think this bloke is the one who broke into my house before. And he might be looking to do it again.'

'And why would a bikie want to break into your house?'

'I don't friggin' well know,' Walker hissed. 'Just get your arse up here behind me. He'll be coming through the back window, like before.' Darling hesitated and he added, 'And he might be armed. He'll just as soon as shoot you as me, you know.'

At that, Darling climbed to his feet uneasily and loosened his jacket as he came up behind Walker. 'You go first,' he whispered.

Walker rolled his eyes and shook his head. 'If you insist, chicken.'

'It's not me he's after. I'd prefer to use you as a human shield than be shot at for some brainless thing you've got yourself involved with.'

Ali Harb quietly pried the timber window upward, just like he'd done before, and peered into the dark kitchen. The house was silent but Walker was inside, for sure. All he had to do was to get his grand-mère's amulet back then everything would be right again. Since he'd lost it, the world had fallen apart. The cops had caught Naim, and the other fools had stupidly tried to kidnap someone. At least one of them was dead and the other, the pilot, had no idea who Ali was. And so far, Naim had not squawked to the coppers. If he did, he'd be dead meat, in jail or out of it, and he was sure Naim knew it. He could count on his silence. And he'd gotten all the smack off his hands. His Brothers had distributed the lot of it. By now most of it would've been injected into junkies all the way from Kings Langley to Kings Cross. Nothing tied him to the drugs or the murders. Nothing except his lucky amulet. If he could get it back, he would be safe and things would be right for him again.

Ali stepped up onto an old rickety chair, which he'd pulled over from near the back door, and heaved his considerable bulk through the narrow window. The timber chair creaked. The window was a tight fit and he gave another shove. With a mighty crack, the chair collapsed into a pile of splinters, leaving him hanging half in and half out of the kitchen, his legs kicking against the brick wall. His belly was stuck on the sill and his hips were wedged on each side. He flailed one arm forward looking for the edge of the kitchen bench but his hand connected with a bottle, causing it to fly across the room, cracking into pieces on the tiled floor.

He heard a click and bright light blinded him.

His hand finally found the edge of the bench and he hung there, stuck, with his legs outside as he craned his head up. In the doorway was Christopher Walker wearing a dressing gown and not much else. There was someone behind him in the hallway.

'What are you doing?' asked Walker with a baffled look.

Ali was impressed at how calm he sounded; inquisitive rather than afraid or angry.

'What does it look like,' growled Ali, trying to sound intimidating. Somehow, he had to salvage the situation or at least minimise the embarrassment.

'It looks like you're trying to break into my house again but you're too fat to fit through the window,' said Walker.

'The bloody chair broke,' he snapped. 'What sort of rubbish equipment do you have around here?'

Walker moved closer. 'Sorry. I should be more thoughtful. I'll start buying furniture to accommodate fat-arse thieves in future.'

'I'm not a thief.'

'But you agree that you're a fat-arse.'

'Shut up!' Ali tried to make his voice sound menacing. 'I'll tell you what's going to happen. I'm gonna push myself back out then I'm gonna leave. Don't give me any strife or I'll beat the living shit out of you.'

Walker seemed to ignore the threat and came up close. 'What's that on the back of your jacket? Is that a bikie patch?'

'Bloody oath it is,' said Ali. 'So don't cause me any trouble.' He noticed the other fellow had remained in the doorway. His hand was in his jacket, as if he might have a gun. He recognised him as one of the cops who'd been investigating the murders.

'Oh, I wasn't thinking of causing any trouble,' said Walker. 'I'm just interested in why you keep trying to break into my house but not steal anything. Are you a relative of one of my patients?'

'No! Why would I break in for that?'

'Don't know. If you're not a relative then what do you want?'

Ali hesitated. Should he push off and make a run for it? But if he did, he might never get his amulet back. 'You've got something that belongs to me.'

'You? What would I have of yours?' Then a look of realisation came over Walker's face. 'Are you Lebanese?' he asked quickly.

'What if I am?'

'Muslim? I did find a pendant with a prayer written on it in Arabic.' Walker turned to Darling who had now come into the kitchen, and then back at him again. 'If it's yours, you'd know it.'

'It's mine,' he gasped. 'I want it back.'

'Describe it. And tell me what the prayer is.'

'It's silver. From my grand-mère. The prayer is from the Quran. Ayat al-Kursi.'

'Can you recite it?'

'I'm not going to recite it.'

'Well, then you won't get it back.'

'If I recite it, will you give it to me?'

'Maybe. Depends on how well you do. Can you remember it?'

'Of course I can.' He wanted to say that he prayed it every night before he went to sleep but he stopped himself.

'Go on then.'

'Do you speak Arabic?'

'No.'

'How will you know what I say is right?'

Walker pursed his lips. 'I reckon I can tell.'

Ali let out a frustrated breath then began to recite the poem in Arabic. When he was halfway through, Walker held up his hand.

'All right, I believe you.' He dug into the pocket of his dressing-gown and drew out the amulet. 'There you go. It's yours.'

Ali felt a wave of relief come over his body as he received the silver pendant into his rough palm. He couldn't believe his luck! He'd got his grand-mere's precious gift back without having to resort to violence.

'That's very good,' he blurted. 'Thank you.' He meant it. He hung for a few more moments in silence, with the two men staring at him. Then he raised his arms to them.

'Are you gonna help me out?'

CHAPTER FOUR

WALKER AND DARLING heaved on the bikie's arms and at first, there was no movement.

'Pull harder,' yelled the bulky Arab.

They both gave a tug and he popped through like a cork onto the kitchen bench then onto the floor and all three landed in a heap. Walker's dressing-gown came askew. As they climbed to their feet, grunting and groaning and straightening their clothes, there was a knock at the front door.

'Who's that?' asked Darling.

'Beats me,' said Walker. He addressed the bikie. 'Expecting any of your friends?'

'No.'

Walker raised his eyebrow at Darling, but he shook his head.

'What's your name anyway?' asked Walker.

'Ali,' he said, carefully placing the amulet into his jacket pocket.

Walker headed for the hallway and Darling followed. Standing in the open doorway was a man holding a leather briefcase. He was mostly bald, with ears that stuck out, and he had overly large lips.

'Can I help you?' Walker called out.

'The door was unlocked,' he said in a cultured voice. 'I hope you don't mind.' He looked down at the handle. 'Did you know your lock's broken?'

Walker reached the door. 'I'm not interested in whatever you're selling.'

The man looked surprised. 'I'm not selling anything.'

'Well, I don't want to be saved either.'

He shook his head. 'I'm not an evangelist.'

'What are you then?'

He appeared flustered. 'Well, I'm a school teacher, but that doesn't matter. What matters is my brother. He is … was … a geologist.'

Walker frowned. 'Geologist?'

'In PNG. He was killed.' He licked his large lips. 'Well, I think he was killed. Murdered.'

Darling had come up behind Walker. 'Are you saying your brother was Alf Runsack, the geologist who disappeared in the Purosa district six years ago?'

'I'm Peter Runsack, Alf's younger brother.'

Walker nodded. 'Yes, I can see the family resemblance.'

'And you say he was murdered?' said Darling.

'I'm sure of it. And I have proof.' He lifted his briefcase to his chest and patted it. 'Or at least a motive. You know … for why someone would kill him.'

Walker looked back over his shoulder. Ali's bulky form filled the narrow hallway behind Darling. He turned back to Runsack. 'Not here.' He guided him out onto the street. 'Do you know the Lord Nelson?'

'Of course.'

'We'll meet you there in ten. Find a table.'

Walker watched him walk away with rising trepidation. What if he revealed things he didn't want to know? Alf, the missing brother, had known Felicity. Maybe Runsack had evidence of things that were best forgotten. He considered trying to talk Darling out of coming with him, but one glance at his face told him there was no chance. Wendy would speak to Runsack, with or without him.

Walker made his way back into the house as Ali was coming out of the front door.

Ali gave a small deferential bow. 'Thank you for returning my talisman. I owe you a debt.'

Walker was struck by the seriousness of the man. 'No problem. It's clearly yours. I'm just glad it's back with its rightful owner.'

Again, Ali nodded solemnly. 'Others would not have given it up so freely.'

Walker didn't know what else to say. He stood aside as Ali passed. 'Good luck!'

'You will see me again,' he said.

Walker grimaced after the bikie. 'I bloody well hope not,' he muttered.

'Got yourself a new friend,' said Darling.

'I'll go up and change. Wait for me.'

The Lord Nelson Pub was a large sandstone building on the corner of Kent and Argyle Streets frequented by tourists and young men on pub crawls, and Walker and Darling reached it in a few minutes. Large black print above the door declared it to be 'Sydney's Oldest Hotel' although Walker knew of at least three other pubs in the area that claimed the same title.

'Why here?' asked Darling.

Walker normally went to the Hero of Waterloo near his house except when he and Darling had business to attend to, in which case they used the Captain Cook.

'Tourist pub. Unlikely to have anyone unsavoury listening to our conversation.'

'Fair enough,' agreed Darling. 'Anyone at the Cook is just as likely a snitch, a crook or a cop.'

'Or all three at once,' said Walker. Darling let out a short laugh.

Just before they went in, Darling pulled Walker up by placing his hand on his arm. 'Just to warn you, I'm going to ask questions about Felicity.'

Walker studied his old friend's face – olive skin, dark eyes with thick black brushes above. 'That's your prerogative, Wendy. But you know what, you've already accused me of eating her dead body. I don't think you can say or do anything else that will hurt me.' He turned away and walked through the pub door.

'Except prove it,' he heard Darling say behind him.

Peter Runsack was sitting at a table near the far wall and Darling made his way there, while Walker stopped at the bar to order three schooners. While he waited for them to be poured, Walker looked around the sandstone-walled room. The place was half-full with patrons sitting at tables or at the bar, most of them tourists by Walker's reckoning. At a table near the door was a group of loud English tourists who were comparing the Nelson's lager to the brew from their local in Manchester. Beside Runsack's table was a white-haired fellow sitting by himself and on the other side were two young women sharing a bottle of white.

Walker's gaze moved to Alf Runsack's brother. Just the sight of him brought back memories of the last few days with Felicity in New Guinea. They had just finished a tour of the villages in the Purosa district and were making their way back to the Misapi Mission with Alf. But something else had happened. Walker struggled to remember his last meeting with the geologist. It was the day before Felicity drowned … they'd got separated … something terrible had happened. Walker closed his eyes. There was a feeling of impending danger, but it was coming from behind – they were being chased. They weren't paying attention to the rising river, the torrential downpour. Then the flood had come, washing them away. But just before the water hit them, Walker recalled looking back and seeing them – the ones who were chasing them.

He opened his eyes.

Runsack sat with a long serious face and prominent ears, his spindly legs pulled up beneath the table, reminding Walker of a Praying Mantis. He clutched his briefcase to his chest as if it might be stolen at any minute.

Walker took the beers to the table and sat down, the memory of that fatal day fading from his mind with each step. His left hand still felt clumsy but he could carry the three beers, although he had to concentrate.

Runsack took a long sip of his beer before he spoke. 'As I told you, my brother, Alf, was a geologist working for the Australian government.'

Walker nodded. 'I knew him. He was working in the same area as me in PNG. I was training the local health workers about TB checks. Alf was doing a report about oil. It had been discovered in the western highlands and people thought it might be found in the Eastern Highlands as well. We travelled together …' He stopped abruptly and took a sip of this beer. He didn't want to talk about Felicity.

'That's right,' said Peter. 'He was doing a report for the PNG government.'

Walker screwed up his forehead in thought. 'From memory, Alf said there was no oil. He was on his way back to give his report. Then he disappeared.' He studied Alf's brother's face carefully, trying to remember.

Runsack became excited. 'He said that? He said that there was no oil? Are you sure?'

Walker was disturbed at his intensity. 'Maybe. Why's it so important?'

He tapped the briefcase on his lap. 'I have evidence of the same. Alf's report. He sent me a copy.'

Walker looked at Darling then back at Runsack. 'So?'

'So that's not what the PNG government say. They say that Alf's report confirmed the high likelihood of oil in the Eastern Highlands.'

'That doesn't make sense,' said Walker. 'Why would they say that?'

'Not sure,' said Runsack. 'But I have my suspicions.'

'About what?'

'I've been there and seen it with my own eyes. I was searching for evidence about Alf, why he might have disappeared. There are oil companies there already.' He turned his long face from Walker to Darling. 'And I asked myself, why? Why would oil companies be searching the Eastern Highlands when Alf's report said there was no oil there?'

'So what did you do?' asked Darling.

'I questioned them. I went to Port Moresby and demanded to see the minister. Initially they refused. Kept putting me off, saying he was too busy or was away. Then I told them I had proof. I told them I had a copy of Alf's report. He'd posted it to me from Okapa. Took a few months to arrive but it finally did – after he'd disappeared. At first I didn't understand. Why would he send me a report? I'm not a geologist. But then later I realised – it was proof, in case they tried to change it. And they did! The minister showed me his version of the report. It was different; it concluded there was a high likelihood of oil in the highlands. I told the minister it was wrong, that it had been changed. He didn't believe me. He wanted to see my copy but I didn't have it with me. I'd left it back in Australia. Safe.' He tapped his briefcase. 'He threw me out of his office. His thugs accompanied me to the airport and I was bundled onto the next flight home.'

Walker stared at the man for a few moments then took a gulp of his beer. 'So why are you telling me? What do I have to do with it?'

'But you already said it! Alf told you there was no oil. You can back up the report. You can say it was a lie.'

'I don't know about that,' said Walker, raising his palms. 'I'm not sure I want to get involved.'

Runsack shook his head in disbelief. 'Involved? But you *are* involved. You were one of the last people to see my brother alive.' He put both hands down on to the table. 'Which brings me to my next question.' He leaned forward and looked at Walker directly. 'You must tell me the truth. Do you know what happened to my brother? Was he murdered?'

Walker's face was blank. 'I don't know. I can't remember.'

'You were seen leaving Purosa with him. You and your wife and a guide.'

He shook his head dumbly. 'My wife died. Drowned. The guide drowned too. I almost died.' He re-focused on

Runsack. 'Maybe your brother was drowned in the same flood?'

'Were you with him?'

Walker rubbed his eyes, trying to dredge up lost memories. 'I don't think so. I think something had happened to him. Someone … some people were following us. I think they meant to hurt us. I think … I think they hurt Alf.' He raised his face. 'I remember a man with a machete.'

'Where?'

He closed his eyes, struggling to remember. 'South of Misapi Mission. South-west of Purosa. They were chasing us. We were running from them … they were going to kill us. Then the flood came.'

Darling grabbed Walker's arm. 'Why haven't you told me this before?'

He faced Darling. 'Sometimes I don't know what is real and what's my imagination. But now I remember. They were chasing us the day Flea drowned. We all got washed down the river in the flood.'

'My brother as well?'

'No. Alf had left us earlier that morning, heading back to Purosa. Different direction.'

Darling shook his arm. 'Are you sure? Are you sure Flea drowned? *You* didn't drown, and she was a good swimmer. Do you think the men could've caught her? She had a hole in her skull.'

'Hole in her skull!?' said Walker. 'You never told me that.'

'You never gave me a chance. You've disappeared for almost a week.'

'But you said I ate her,' Walker said, his voice hoarse. He was conscious of the tingling in his hand.

'What!?' demanded Runsack. 'Are you saying they were all eaten by cannibals? That's preposterous.'

'Not your brother,' snapped Darling. 'I didn't find his bones.' He glanced at the surrounding tables then dropped his voice. 'Only Felicity's and the guide's. In a hut in the highlands – the place where Kit was kept. He'd been delirious for weeks before he was found. We dug up two sets of bones; both skulls had holes in them. Kit and his carer — the guide's elderly wife — had no food for over a month, and she was from a generation that practiced funerary rites. The Fore people.'

'Cannibalism in this day and age?' Runsack gasped with disbelief.

Darling opened his hands. 'The local cops thought so.'

'This is ridiculous,' said Runsack. 'I believe my brother was murdered by people trying to cover up his damning report about oil in the highlands. And I think the PNG government, or some part of it, is in on the cover-up. I have evidence of fraud.' He tapped his briefcase. 'I will not let this real evidence be caught up in some horror story about cannibals and witch doctors. I owe it to my brother.'

'I think we've said enough tonight,' said Darling. 'We have a lot to think about. I suggest we get some rest and sleep on it. Where are you staying, Peter?'

'The Holiday Inn on George Street.'

'How about we meet up again tomorrow? I'll call you at the hotel.'

After Runsack had left, Darling asked Walker, 'What are you doing tomorrow, Kit?'

'You never told me about the holes in the skull,' he snapped.

'Like I said, you've disappeared for a week. This is the first time I've seen you.'

'So you wait till we're talking to a total stranger before you tell me?'

'I'm sorry about that. But at least you know.' When Walker remained silent, he said, 'I still have to get a statement from you about the other matter.'

Walker stood abruptly. 'Whatever.' Before Darling could reply, he turned and stalked out of the door.

Darling lingered at the table and watched Walker leave. Maybe he should have told him about the skull earlier. But he hadn't a chance. And Walker had kept things from him as well. Why wait until now to reveal that people had been chasing them before the flood? It just didn't add up. There was something fishy about Walker's story. And Runsack's story was equally unbelievable.

He looked around the room with growing unease. There was something about this pub that made him uncomfortable. Most of the room had cleared. The English tourists were gone. A well-built blond man had been sitting at the next table and had left about ten minutes before. Darling had marked him as a foreigner, with neat clothes and straight back and, incongruently, a metal stud in the septum of his nose just above his lips, like a punk rocker. He had spent most of the time sipping on a liqueur and reading the paraphernalia about Horatio Nelson on the pub wall. He would have been able to hear their conversation. Two girls, one dark-skinned, the other white and both dressed casually in shorts and canvas shoes, had been at the next table all evening. They were still there with their heads together, giggling and drinking wine. If anything, they looked too sweet and innocent.

Then he laughed at himself. *What am I doing? I'm suspicious of everyone.* Maybe he needed a holiday.

With a sigh, he finished his drink then made his way to the door.

CHAPTER FIVE

THE NEXT MORNING, Walker awoke in dim light after having had – for the first time in a long while – a restful sleep unhampered by dreams. It was as if the catharsis of the last week had finally given him some respite. Feeling unusually energetic, he rolled out of bed, threw open the French doors and stepped onto the balcony. It was still cool and the streets were deserted. He glanced back through the door at his bedside clock – 5.30 am! His eyes drifted to the rumpled bed, his prison for the last week.

'Bugger that!'

He quickly donned shorts and a T-shirt, then slipped on a battered pair of Nike running shoes and thumped down the stairs and onto the street where he stood hanging onto his front fence while he stretched his quads. He was never certain that stretching did anything but all the other joggers seemed to do it, so he felt he should look the part.

He started jogging jauntily down the hill towards the water, breathing the cool air in deeply, feeling the best he had in a long while. The running was easy despite not having exercised for months and he figured that possibly he possessed some sort of natural fitness. He got to the end of Lower Fort and skipped down the stone steps to Hickson Road, coming out near the recently opened Pier One Restaurant – an upmarket establishment that sat at the end of a row of disused warehouses at Walsh Bay. He jogged more slowly along Hickson beside the old warehouses, which were currently undergoing refurbishment. There was talk of restaurants and maybe apartments. One of the wharf buildings had been taken over by the Sydney Theatre Company a few years before. Despite the flat ground, he began to feel sweaty and more than a little puffed, so he stopped before a poster on the outside of the building which boasted the next theatre production, starting in April – *Racing Demons*. 'Some sort of religious rubbish,' he muttered to himself. 'Can't see myself going to that.'

As he stood catching his breath, two figures came out of the covered passage that led to the theatre company and jogged away along Hickson Road. They were both young women, skimpily clad in running gear that showed off long legs, one set white and the other dark. Walker recognised them as the two women from the Lord Nelson the night before. Maybe they were locals but he didn't think so. He knew most of the people in the area and young women like that were unlikely to move into a dumpy suburb like Millers Point. *Tourists probably*.

He waited until they were out of sight then jogged across the road to a narrow opening between the multi-storey historic red-brick buildings. A sandstone arch above declared the gap to be the 'Ferry Steps' and he began his way up. Soon he was puffing and after a few more steps he had to stop running and haul himself up using the handrail. He had to stop twice and was glad there was no one around to see him gasping and coughing. Finally, he reached the top at Pottinger Street and he leaned forward, hands on knees, struggling to catch his breath.

'So much for natural fitness,' he grunted.

He walked slowly the rest of the way home, hands on hips, breathing deeply until the dizziness finally subsided, vowing that this year he would get fitter. Maybe he'd join a gym.

After a long shower and a quick breakfast, he jumped into his BMW and made his way to Western Meadows with the top down, trying not to think about the one person he did not want to talk to – Angela Chee.

Instead of heading for work in Parramatta, Barry Darling drove his Commodore from Glebe to the city, beating the worst of the traffic and promptly finding a parking spot near the Holiday Inn on George Street just after 7 am. It had only taken ten minutes, much better than the forty-minute slog across town to Parramatta, and he briefly considered asking for a transfer to the local Rocks Station. *Maybe if I'm lucky getting that house*, he said to himself but knew it was an excuse. He was comfortable at Parramatta and wasn't keen on starting all over again at a new station.

He made his way to the concierge and waited while Runsack's room was called. When the phone was not answered, he made a search through the restaurant where guests were breakfasting, but there was no sign of the man.

'Maybe he's out for breakfast,' suggested the concierge when Darling enquired again. 'There's a few places up the road.'

He decided to have a look in the first few but if he didn't find him, he'd head off and see if he could catch him in the evening. Runsack's story of political intrigue was a bit out of Darling's comfort zone. He realised he'd have to refer the matter on but baulked at the idea of passing such an interesting case to his boss in head office. He and Senior Detective Sergeant Royce Wills did not exactly see eye to eye, especially after Royce had made a fool of himself in the recent murder case at Western Meadows.

As Darling made his way out of the front door of the hotel, he paused as two young women clad in meagre jogging gear came through in the opposite direction. He held the door open for them, realising they were from the pub the night before. He moved through the door, glancing back at their shapely bare legs and collided with someone coming through behind them. The fellow was solid and Darling could sense his strength when he grabbed him around the shoulders to prevent them both from falling.

'So sorry,' came an accented voice – South African. 'I do apologise.'

His face was close and Darling recognised the metal stud in the nose. The blond man smiled, showing white teeth, and gestured politely to allow Darling to pass. He mumbled his own apology and moved away, head down, feeling embarrassed, realising he shouldn't have been gawking at the girls so openly. Lucky, they didn't know he was a copper!

Feeling flustered, Darling decided to give up the idea of finding Runsack and made his way back to his car. He drove up George Street then realised he'd have to pass Kit's house, noting as he did that his car was gone.

As he sat in traffic waiting to turn onto the main carriageway out of the city, a call came over the radio: a body had been found in the harbour at Walsh Bay. Circumstances were suspicious.

Darling sat for a few moments contemplating the message. It had nothing to do with him. The Rocks coppers would look after it. He had a pile of things to do at the office. The locals wouldn't want him sticking his nose into their business.

The light ahead turned green.

'Bugger!' he spat as he flicked on the siren and turned his car across the oncoming traffic. 'It better not be Runsack!'

It was Runsack. A man walking his dog had found the body face-down in the water next to the pier at the Sydney Theatre Company. The fellow who found him had jumped into the water to try to revive him but had given up when he realised the body was cold and dead. The failed rescuer now stood nearby, wrapped in a blanket, his cocker spaniel sitting obediently at his feet, while one of the local police took a statement.

The Water Police were fishing the body out of the water and as it flopped onto the gunwale, Darling could see clearly it was Runsack. There was no sign of a briefcase.

CHAPTER SIX

AN HOUR LATER, Darling was sitting in the office of the superintendent of The Rocks Police Station. Fred Bowles had aged since Darling had last seen him over two decades ago when, as a sergeant in this very office, he'd hauled Kit and him over the coals for car stealing. He had threatened to send them both to Cobham Juvenile Justice Centre if they didn't change their ways. It was Bowles who'd led Darling to join the force. He'd scared the living daylights out of them. Darling suspected it had also caused Kit Walker to get serious at school. The threat of failure had driven them both, although in different directions – one into law enforcement and the other into medicine.

Bowles had always seemed huge but now Darling realised he was only slightly taller than him. He was certainly bigger in other ways: the belly that rolled out over his belt, the jowls. And his personality was still as expansive as ever.

'Young Barry! So, you kept your word. Well done, boy! Would've been a terrible waste for you to spend time.'

Darling smiled weakly. 'I have to thank you again, Fred. You saved my arse.'

Bowles nodded, his jowls wobbling. 'So I did, so I did. Now how can I help you?'

'It's about the stiff in the harbour.'

He raised his eyebrows. 'The one at Walsh Bay?'

Darling tried not to react. Was there more than one? 'Yes. I know him. I met him last night at the Lord Nelson.'

'You don't say. Who was he?'

'Name's Peter Runsack. He wanted me to help investigate his brother's murder.'

'Oh?'

'Or suspected murder. Alf Runsack was a geologist who was looking for evidence of oil in the highlands of New Guinea when he disappeared about six years ago.'

'You don't say? Do you think the deaths are related?'

'Not sure. But Runsack – Peter – was talking about some serious stuff last night. Claimed the PNG government had tried to suppress a report that would've affected foreign funding. Runsack reckons it got his brother killed.'

Bowles nodded slowly, encouraging Darling to continue.

'Reckons he had proof. Had it in a briefcase that he was carrying with him. I was at the scene this morning. There was no briefcase.'

'Could be in his room.'

Darling nodded. 'Or at the bottom of the harbour.' He leaned forward. 'Or the killer could have it.'

Bowles was silent for a moment. 'Could be a lead. We'll look into it. We'll check the room and get some divers on the scene.'

'You'll keep me in the loop?'

'Sure,' said Bowles. 'Although I'm not sure why. You're based at Parramatta. That's a long way from here. What's wrong? They don't give you enough work out there?'

'Personal interest. Runsack did come to me first.'

Bowles examined him for a few more moments before smiling. 'I think I can do that, Bazza. I'll let you know.' He opened his arms expansively. 'But tell me, what about Kit? I hear he's a doctor. Somewhere out in the Western Suburbs. But that's not too bad. He's a clever boy. I'm sure if he works hard, he'll get himself a place in a proper hospital one day, like Prince Alfred or St Vincent's.' He raised a stubby finger. 'Application. Application and hard work. That's what counts. And honesty. Application, hard work and being honest. If Kit does all those things, one day he'll be able to work at one of Sydney's best hospitals, no worries.'

Darling nodded silently. He wondered for a moment whether he should stand up for his old friend but decided against it. 'His wife died. Felicity – you remember her.'

'Yes, I heard something about that. Poor little Flea, she was such a sweet girl. She and Kit suited each other.'

Darling flinched inwardly and his next words were terse. 'She died in New Guinea under his watch. Drowned. He didn't look after her.'

Bowles leaned back in his chair and studied his face carefully. 'You don't say? I heard she was caught up in a flash flood, and that Kit almost died too.' He leaned forward and held Darling's eyes in his. 'Sounds like you hold a grudge.'

Darling began to regret his snide remark and looked away into the front room where the young constables were working at various desks.

Bowles continued. 'You were hot on her as well, weren't you, Barry? Dated her for a while, if I'm not mistaken.' He continued to examine Darling as if he were an exhibit in a court case. 'You sure you're not letting your feelings get in the way of your judgement?'

He squirmed in his seat and refused to look at his former mentor.

'So, what do you think?' Bowles persisted. 'You think Kit let his wife die? Or worse? You think he killed her maybe?'

Darling stood up, his fists tight against his sides. 'No!' he shouted. 'No, none of those things.'

Policemen in the other room were staring at him through the glass. He lowered his voice. 'But he should've looked after her. That's all I'm saying. If I ...' His shoulders slumped and he looked away again.

'I?' Bowles spat. 'What? *You* would've saved her, if you were there?' He looked indignant. '*You* would've been able to pluck her from a flooded river when Kit couldn't, even though he's a better swimmer than you, ten times over? Or what? You'd have drowned to sacrifice yourself so she would live?' Bowles shook his large head. 'Get real, Barry. Use your brain. I know you've got one but the way you're talking you'd think it's full of shit.'

Darling bowed his head but Bowles was relentless.

'You *are* full of shit. Shit-for-brains. Is that you? You and Kit were the best of friends. But when his wife died, instead of comforting him like a true friend, you blamed him. I've heard all about it. Blamed him for his wife's death when no one could've stopped it.' He slowly got to his feet, his face as dark as thunderclouds. 'The more I think of it, the more I'm disgusted. Weak. Weak and gutless. Weak, gutless and selfish.' He slumped his considerable bulk back into his chair. 'You should be ashamed of yourself.'

'I didn't come here to be insulted,' Darling said tersely.

'Why *did* you come here then? Trying to muscle in on our murder investigation. What? Are you such a hot-shot? Think you can do a better job than us, is that it?'

His shoulders slumped. 'No, Fred, not at all. I never would. I owe you everything. It's just ...'

'You think this bloke's murder might have something to do with Felicity's death?' said Bowles.

Darling nodded slowly. 'It might do. Runsack's brother was with Felicity and Kit just before he disappeared. Maybe they were caught up in it somehow.'

Bowles continued to stare at him without speaking until Darling slumped back down in the chair. His expression softened. 'Okay, Barry, I'll keep you in the loop.' He raised an admonishing finger. 'But if I think you're getting obsessed or making stupid decisions, I'll cut you off, you hear me?'

'Thanks, Fred. I promise I'll be sensible.

'And try and make up with Kit, for fuck's sake.'

'That I can't promise. I think ... I think a lot of water has flowed under the bridge.'

'Try for my sake, at least.'

Darling's voice was quiet. 'I'll try.'

CHAPTER SEVEN

WALKER ARRIVED LATE to work and parked in the doctors' carpark then made his way to his office. He'd been AWOL for over a week and hadn't contacted anyone about it. People deserved an explanation. Who would have looked after his patients? The two other oncologists in the department were as overworked as he was, which meant they probably would've left the day-to-day care to his advanced trainee. Walker felt his guts twist as he thought about it.

Angela Chee.

What was he going to do about her?

Her father had been murdered and she'd been the prime suspect. In the end, she was innocent of the murder, but she'd considered it. She'd admitted to Walker that she'd contemplating killing her father for what he'd done to her mother. Was that wrong? It wasn't against the law; you couldn't throw someone in jail for thinking about killing someone if they didn't go through with it. But was it wrong?

As far as he could remember, you weren't supposed to covet your neighbours' goods or his wife or ox or something. So according to the church, just thinking about it was wrong. But when it came to killing, the commandments were definite. 'Thou shalt not kill'. Moses said nothing about *thinking* about killing. The whole thing didn't make any sense.

But the worse thing was that Angela had found out he'd been sleeping with Cassie.

Walker shook his head as he wandered along the hospital corridor. *What am I going to do?* He liked Angela. Maybe more than liked. He squeezed his eyes shut and pushed his knuckle into his forehead until it hurt. Why did he have to sleep with Cassie?

'Whoa, big boy!' said a female voice in his ear. He snapped his eyes open to see a large face close to his and he reeled backwards. 'You've got to watch where you're going, Chris. Almost smacked right into me.'

'Sorry, Marcia. I've not been feeling very well.'

Marcia Links was the Palliative Care consultant for the hospital, three decades older than him, overweight and ruddy-faced. A retired general practitioner, she looked after the terminally ill patients in a nearby hospice and undertook consultations at Western Meadow.

'So I've heard,' said Marcia. 'Everything all right now? You look terrible. But you often do, so that's no indicator.' She looked him up and down. 'I hear you saved your registrar's life by heave-hoing that helicopter doc over the cliff. Well done! He got what was coming to him.'

Walker was dismayed. 'Is that what people are saying?'

'Something like that. Maybe no one's actually said you pushed him but I can put two and two together.' She tapped the side of her bulbous nose with her index finger. 'Don't worry, Chris, I don't think less of you. You and I both know how cheap life is. The good die young and the bastards live forever. It's good to see one of those bastards get what he deserves for a change.'

Dumbfounded, Walker glanced up and down the corridor to make sure no patients were around to overhear and was relieved they were alone. He didn't know how to reply. Finally, he squeezed out a weak, 'Thanks,' as he attempted to sidestep his colleague.

But Marcia moved to block him and him found himself staring at a gold fish pendant wedged between her considerable cleavage. 'And another thing, you have to do something about your mate, Holland S. Xavier.' She exaggerated the 'S' as if she was hissing at the villain at a Christmas pantomime. 'Tell him to stop treating people to within an inch of their grave. Enough's enough. If he had his way, he'd still be pumping his patients full of chemo long after their souls have left their cold bodies.'

He raised his hands. 'Sure, sure. I'll speak to him.' It was a running argument between the two consultants and Walker felt like he was always the meat in the sandwich. 'We should have a meeting about it.' This time he managed to squeeze past.

'Just tell him,' she called as he raced away. He waved his arm in the air but didn't look back.

When he finally got to the outpatient clinic in the radiation oncology department, Angela had already started without him. He'd turned up unannounced and the clinic nurses were unusually quiet for a change. It was clear from their whispers and guarded looks that they knew the whole story. Maybe they thought he was a murderer.

Walker flicked through the pile of patient files on the desk, looking to see what sort of clinic it was to be. The list wasn't as long as he expected and he suspected a lot of patients had been cancelled on the assumption he wasn't turning up.

Angela came into the common area scribbling in a file, looking hassled. Her hair was held up in a ponytail, she'd no makeup on and there were dark smudges under her eyes. Her skin had lost its normal glow.

'Dr Walker,' she said stiffly when she saw him, stopping at the door. Walker wasn't sure whether he sensed coldness or uncertainty. 'Are you ...' she hesitated and glanced at the nurses who looked on unashamedly. 'Are you okay? You haven't been here for a week.'

'Sorry about that,' Walker said awkwardly, conscious of the nurses' stares. He'd been uncontactable for a week with no excuse and Angela would've borne the brunt of the workload. 'Have the clinics been busy?' *Of course they would've been busy and Angela would've had to care for the inpatients as well!*

'No, not too bad.'

'You owe her one, Dr Walker,' interjected one of the nurses, a tubby Filipino. 'Angela has been working like a dog without anyone to help.' Then she smiled. 'You need to take her out to dinner again.' She giggled. 'Lots of food and wine.'

'Yes,' said another, joining in with a cheeky smile. 'You two need to kiss and make up.' The nurses chortled.

Walker walked closer to Angela and dropped his voice. 'I wasn't feeling well. I'm sorry.'

Angela remained still, emotionless. 'That's understandable. You had a shock.' She looked away and opened the file she was holding. 'We'd better get on with the clinic. We've got lots of inpatients to see after this.'

The clinic took two hours and was undertaken largely in stilted silence with the two interacting only for professional concerns. Angela kept her questions short and infrequent and Walker mostly answered with a yes or a no. The nurses appeared to sense the tension and went about their work in hushed tones, making silent faces at each other.

Finally they were alone, walking together towards the ward but still they remained silent. Then Walker said, 'You have every right to not want to work with me. Everything I've done ...'

'I've been thinking of requesting a transfer to the other team,' she said.

He grunted. When it was clear she wasn't going to say anything more, he said, 'It wasn't right of me to not turn up without an explanation.'

'Yes,' agreed Angela. She walked further before speaking. 'I came round to your house. I knocked but there was no answer.'

'I wasn't well.'

'Obviously,' she snapped. 'A normal person doesn't lock himself away for days and ignore his friends. Only someone with something very wrong with them would do that.'

'Wrong with me! You told Blinkton to wait for me to turn up, then kill me instead of you.' He turned to face her. 'I heard you on the cliff top.'

Angela looked shocked. 'I didn't —'

'You did!' He looked away again.

She clenched her teeth with anger. 'How dare you! You were sleeping with Cassie when you said you wanted to be with me.'

He stopped. 'I'm sorry.'

She turned back. 'Sorry? Sorry you slept with her or sorry you were caught?'

When he failed to answer, she let out a frustrated sound. 'What do you want, Chris? I just wish you'd make up your mind.'

He shook his head despondently and started walking again. 'I don't know. Too many things have happened. Felicity's death, your father's murder. What happened at The Gap.' He glanced at her. 'You going off with Blinkton.'

She made an exasperated noise.

He dropped his voice. 'But the thing that really got me is what Wendy said. What he said I did with Felicity's body.'

They approached the elevator and one of the wardsmen held the door for them. They ascended in silence, then they were alone again. The ward was ahead, which would be full of buzzing nurses and interns and beds of patients with problems.

Before they reached the door, Angela stopped and turned to him. 'Did you, Chris? Did you do what Detective Darling said?'

Walker examined her face and saw not ghoulish curiosity or abhorrence but concern.

Her voice became a whisper. 'Did you do it?' She tightened her lips and swallowed as if she might be sick. 'Did you eat her flesh?'

He looked down at his feet. 'I don't know. I really don't know.' He raised a face creased with anguish. 'But I remember something else. I remember we were being chased. I think someone was trying to kill us.'

'Kill you?'

A coarse voice interrupted them. 'What are you two whispering about?'

Walker swung around to see Marcia Links standing over them. He thought he caught a whiff of alcohol.

'Don't you two get all lovey-dovey here on the ward, you'll get all the nurses in a lather.' She coughed out a raucous laugh.

'We're just about to start a ward round,' snapped Walker. He strode off to the nurses' station with Angela close behind.

Marcia stood at the entrance to the ward. 'Remember what I said about Holland,' she rasped.

Walker ignored her.

CHAPTER EIGHT

HOLLAND S. XAVIER was at the nurses' station when Walker arrived and he greeted him in an uncharacteristically friendly fashion. Holland was about a decade older than Walker and was tall and thin with wavy brown hair down to his collar. He favoured striped suits with a vest and pocket handkerchief and he spoke with a cultivated Australian accent, typical of the private Eastern Suburbs schools of the sixties. Holland had spent some time training in London and he'd adopted the English boarding school manner of some of his peers.

'Ah, Walker,' he called. 'Glad you're here. Having a spot of bother with one of my patients. I was hoping you could give me a hand.'

'Sure, Holland, how can I help?'

He came closer and rocked back and forth on his patent leather shoes, one arm behind his back as he fiddled with his tie with the other. 'It's that damned banshee, Marcia Links. She's on the warpath and I think it's my scalp she has in her sights.'

Walker's heart sank. It looked like he was going to be dragged into this whether he liked it or not. 'Oh, and what can I do?'

'It's about one of my patients, Mr Peter Shore. Small cell lung cancer who's failed first-line carbo and etoposide and then second-line treatment. Normally I'd call it quits but the patient and his son will have none of it. They're both demanding more treatment. I was considering using single-agent doxorubicin, with verapamil as an MDR-1 inhibitor.'

Walker didn't answer immediately. He knew further chemotherapy would almost certainly be futile in this situation. Holland had done his PhD in chemotherapy resistance with the multi-drug resistance protein, called MDR-1, that allowed the cancer cells to pump out chemotherapy to avoid injury. Verapamil was a drug commonly used for heart problems and had been shown to block MDR-1 in cell models. But being effective in highly-controlled cell culture experiments was a long way from use in a human. Walker thought the chances of it working were slim. On the other hand, he'd also been in the position where desperate patients refused to give up.

'I suppose so,' he said slowly. 'If the patient is insisting and knows the chance of response is low.'

'My words exactly,' answered Holland. 'But Links is on my back to withdraw. I was hoping you would see the patient and give an opinion. Back me up.'

Walker looked at this watch. 'Now? I'm not sure I've —'

'I would appreciate it,' he insisted. 'I'll owe you one. I did cover for you last week, in case you weren't aware of it.'

Walker was sure Holland would have left the daily care of his patients to Angela but he had to concede he would have been responsible. 'Of course. Thank you, by the way. I wasn't well.'

Holland continued to smile expectantly. Walker let out a sigh. 'Where is he?'

'Good man. I was about to visit him now.' He waved his arm towards one of the rooms.

Peter Shore was a stout man in his sixties, sitting in an armchair in a darkened single room, which he had set up like an office. He had a stack of papers on the bedstand and was holding a sheet, making edits in blue pen. A visitor sat adjacent to him as if they had been reading the document together. Apart from being bald, the patient looked remarkably well, despite having come through two rounds of chemotherapy.

'My will,' said Peter, flicking the paper up after he'd been introduced to Walker. 'This is my son, Jason. He's helping me proofread – he's a printer. Knew he'd come in handy one day.' The father and son shared a fond smile.

Walker explained his presence and began to ask a standard history but the patient interrupted.

'Dr Walker, I appreciate you coming but I feel I'm wasting your time.'

The way he said it gave Walker the impression he considered it was his, not Walker's, time being wasted.

'I understand the chance of this next chemotherapy working is very small. I also know there is risk of serious infection and other complications. If you want me to sign something to absolve the hospital of any claim then I'm happy to do so. But I'm of sound mind, I know the risks and I want to try. As I've said to Dr Xavier, I don't want to die without knowing that I've tried every available therapy.'

'Well, it sounds like you don't need me. I can only agree with your course of action.' Walker reached out to shake Peter's hand. 'Good luck.'

He nodded to the son and turned to leave the room but collided with someone coming in. He stepped back. Marcia Links.

'I thought I'd better break in on this secret little meeting you seem to be having,' said Links, pointing to Walker and Holland. She addressed the patient. 'What sort of rubbish have these two been spinning?'

'Sorry, I don't know you,' said Peter.

'Dr Links from Palliative Care. I'm here to stop you from making a mistake.'

Peter frowned and addressed Holland. 'I don't remember us discussing palliative care. I thought our plan was clear. I'm having another try of chemotherapy before I'm shipped off to the death wards.'

'Palliative Care is not terminal care,' corrected Walker. 'If you have complex symptom requirements we often get our Palliative Care team involved, even in people who are curable.

'Do I have complex symptom requirements?' asked Peter of Holland.

He shook his head. 'No, not really. Not at this stage.'

'So why are you here, Dr Links?' asked Peter.

'As I said, to stop you from making a mistake. You should not be offered useless therapy that has a risk of causing serious side effects.'

Jason Shore stood and raised his hand. 'I think there has been a misunderstanding here, doctor. We've been through this in detail with Dr Xavier and now Dr Walker. My father's path is clear. He wants to try the treatment, no matter how low the chances are.'

'Well, you're just a stupid, selfish man who knows nothing about this,' snapped Links. 'Can't you see your father is dying? You should let him do so with dignity.'

The son and father appeared shocked.

Links capitalised on the silence and moved towards the patient. 'Sir, I know it is difficult but you need to let go. You must be given time to go through the stages of dying and you're not going to get there if you're being pumped full of poison. You've obviously been through denial and anger and now you're clearly in the bargaining phase.' She jabbed a thumb at Holland. 'And your doctor should know that. He shouldn't be asking you to make difficult decisions at this time of weakness. He should not be offering a treatment that everyone knows is futile. You just need some time.' She softened her voice. 'Soon you will move through a period of depression but, don't worry, we *will* get you through it. Then finally you will reach a period of acceptance and be able to die peacefully.'

Peter spoke calmly. 'I'm aware of Kubler-Ross's work, Dr Links, but I'm not sure she'd appreciate your over-simplification of the process of dying.'

Links was indignant. 'What? I'll have you know I've shepherded hundreds of patients through the dying process. I know what I'm talking about. And don't tell me about Kubler-Ross.' She held up the gold fish necklace from her breast. 'This was a personal gift from the great woman herself.'

'That may be so but I've decided I want to try another round of chemotherapy, regardless of how futile you may think it is. It's my decision. Just because I don't fit into your neat little boxes is beside the point. Dr Xavier has kindly agreed to help me in any way he can.'

Links' face became suffused with anger and her lips tightened. 'I've had enough of this nonsense.' She stomped from the room.

Walker followed Links, catching up with her in the corridor. 'Marcia, I should let you know that I agree with Holland. The patient is of sound mind. His request is reasonable.'

Links spun around. 'It is *not* reasonable, it's an atrocity. It borders on professional misconduct. I intend to take this further.'

Walker was close enough to smell her breath. 'Marcia, I have to ask, have you been drinking?'

She looked affronted but also flustered. 'Drinking! How dare you! I barely touch the stuff, and definitely not while I'm working. How *dare* you.'

The son, Jason, joined them in the corridor. 'Dr Links, I know you're trying to help but don't you understand that my father will not be able to die peacefully unless he knows he's tried everything possible? He doesn't care much about physical suffering. He wants to be sure that he's not left any therapy that he could've reasonably tried.'

Links drew herself up and raised her face. 'And don't you understand I'm an expert in this area? I know he should not be undertaking futile treatment and that Dr Xavier should not be pushing it.' She waved her finger in the son's face. 'I may not be able to stop your father from being a fool but

I can stop Holland and his fruitless and dangerous practices. Right now, I'm going to medical administration to put a stop to this nonsense.'

Angela had waited patiently for Walker until he was finished with Holland. 'Our intern is on the next ward. He asked whether we can start the round there.'

As they walked along, she remained distant and Walker thought her gait stilted, as if she was making sure they didn't accidentally touch. They reached the next ward to find their large intern, Vince Greenway, waiting for them, leaning against the nurses' station, legs crossed before him, tapping his own patella with a tendon hammer while he chatted with two nurses. They laughed at something he said but he snapped to attention when he saw Walker and Angela approaching.

'I was about to page you again, Angela,' said Vince. 'One of the new admissions, Mrs Sandra Wright, she's not well – breathless and hypotensive. I'm worried she might have had a pulmonary embolism. A Doppler shows she has a DVT in the lower leg. She's already on heparin.'

'You don't look very worried about it,' she said with irritation, glancing at the retreating nurses. 'How low is her BP?'

'Ninety systolic.'

'Ninety! When were you going to call me? When she was dead? Take me to her, quickly.'

Walker noticed how Vince had spoken to Angela in preference to him and how she had taken control, not bothering to defer to him. How long had he been away? A little more than a week, but the way Angela was acting, it could've been months.

Mrs Sandra Wright was a forty-something-year-old woman who lay propped up in bed, her pale face twisted in distress. She had a blood pressure cuff on her right arm. A thin balding man, probably her husband, sat at her side clasping her other hand.

'What's the story,' asked Walker.

Vince spoke quickly. 'Past history of breast cancer five years ago, treated by mastectomy and adjuvant chemo. No recurrence. Now one week of fatigue and a swollen left leg. She became more breathless and dizzy last night and was admitted through Emergency. An ultrasound shows a clot in the lower left leg and they started her on heparin. She was okay overnight but her blood pressure started to drop an hour ago.'

Angela took the woman's hand. 'Mrs Wright, I'm Angela Chee, one of the doctors, and this is Dr Walker, the specialist. Tell me how you're feeling.'

'Exhausted,' said the woman. 'I feel breathless.'

Walker noted that her breathing rate seemed normal. Her lips were not blue but the skin of her face was pale.

'Do you have any pain?' asked Angela. The woman shook her head. 'Any discomfort in the chest?' persisted Angela.

'I don't feel right.' She raised worried eyes to Angela's. 'Do you think I'm having a heart attack?'

'Don't know yet,' murmured Angela, as she felt the woman's pulse in her wrist. 'Thready but regular.' She opened the woman's nightdress and put the stethoscope on her chest next to the breast. 'No murmurs. Faint though.' She moved the stethoscope around and asked the patient to take deep breaths. 'Chest's clear.' She rotated her patient's head gently to the side and examined her neck then frowned. 'JVP is up.' Next, she pumped up the blood pressure cuff and listened with her stethoscope at the elbow as she slowly deflated the cuff. She stopped when the mercury column reached eighty and listened for some moments then slowly let the cuff deflate completely. When she finally stood up her frown had deepened. 'Pulsus paradoxus.'

'We should get cardiology,' said Walker.

Her husband had watched the examination with increasing distress. 'What's wrong with my wife?'

'She has fluid around the heart,' said Walker. 'It's compressing it and making it difficult for it to work.'

'Can you do anything?'

'We have to remove the fluid,' said Angela. 'And we have to do it soon.'

But as they watched, the patient became even paler and her head slowly flopped sideways.

'Sandra!' shouted her husband. He shook her shoulders but she refused to rouse.

'Vince,' shouted Angela. 'Get the crash cart and call an arrest.'

Walker lowered the bed flat and pulled the pillow out from under the woman's head then ripped open her nightgown. She was still breathing.

Within moments, Vince and one of the nurses ran in with an ECG monitor on a trolley. Angela pulled the top drawer open and rifled around, pushing packets from side to side. She snapped on gloves and asked the nurse to crack open a packet that contained a long needle, longer than her hand, and attached it to a large syringe. Walker had already cleaned the unconscious woman's chest with yellow iodine solution.

Angela felt for the 'V' where the ribs came together at the bottom of the sternum and placed the tip of the needle on the skin.

'What are you doing?' screamed the husband.

'She's saving your wife's life,' said Walker firmly. He grabbed the man around the shoulders and escorted him from the room. 'The fluid needs to be removed now. Don't worry, your wife won't feel anything.'

Walker came back in to see Angela insert the needle through the skin, aiming for the left shoulder tip. 'You done this before?' he asked.

'No,' she said, her lips tight. 'Have you?' She stopped pushing and sucked back on the syringe. Getting nothing, she pushed it a bit further then sucked back again.

Blood flooded the syringe.

'Do you think I'm in the heart?' she asked Walker.

'No, that's blood-stained pericardial fluid. Fluid from around the heart. The heparin for the DVT has thinned the blood and probably made it worse.'

She disconnected the syringe from the needle and discharged the fluid into a stainless-steel dish then reattached the syringe and sucked more out just as the arrest team arrived.

The cardiology registrar felt for a pulse in the neck. 'Feels good,' he said. 'Shall we check the BP?'

Sandra's colour was much improved and she started to rouse, moaning and breathing heavily. 'Everything is okay, Sandra,' the cardiology registrar said calmly. 'Dr Chee is just removing some fluid you don't need. Try to lie still if you can. It won't take long.'

'Her pressure's up to ninety,' said the nurse.

Angela sucked out another syringe of fluid then pulled the long needle out, pressing firmly with a cotton swab on the puncture site. A nurse placed a dressing over it and taped it down.

Sandra's eyes opened. 'I feel better,' she whispered. 'Thank you. I can breathe again.'

'We'll have to do more tests,' said Angela, 'but I think we might find the breast cancer has come back.'

'But I've had no lumps,' she said, her voice weak.

'It might have spread to the sac around the heart. The pericardium. We'll test the fluid.'

Sandra nodded and closed her eyes. 'Do what you have to do.'

After the patient had been wheeled away to the coronary care unit, the team gathered in the corridor. Vince scratched his head and stepped from foot to foot. 'Sorry, I should've thought about that. I was thinking about a clot in the lung. She was breathless but her blood gases were okay. Why should that happen with cardiac tamponade?'

'Not sure,' said Walker. 'Both ventricles should be compressed equally. Right heart pressures were up, thus the elevated jugular venous pressure. But most people complain of difficulty breathing.' Walker shrugged his shoulders. 'Ask the cardiologists.'

'Regardless, she was obviously sick and had low BP,' Angela said sternly. 'Don't wait so long before you call for help next time.'

They finished the ward round quickly and Walker and Angela left together. He had the sense that she wanted to say something. At the top of the stairs she paused, and Walker descended a few stairs before he realised and turned back towards her.

She pointed in the other direction. 'I have to go to Emergency to see a patient.'

'Okay,' said Walker, relieved. 'I'll see you later then.' He'd had enough of awkward conversations.

But Angela lingered on the top step. 'Chris, I think we need to talk.'

'What about?'

'Us.'

He felt uneasy. 'Sure. When?'

'This Friday night? I can come to your place.'

Walker thought quickly. What if Cassandra turned up? That'd be complicated. 'The place is a mess. How about we go to a pub?'

Angela shook her head. 'Too noisy. And I don't want to drink, I want to talk. It won't take long.'

He hesitated.

'What? Are you going out with Cassie that night? Sleeping with her again?'

He waved his hands. 'No, no. That's not it.'

A door banged below them and someone could be heard on the steps, coming up to their level.

Walker dropped his voice. 'It just sounds so ominous.'

'Not at all. We just need to set things straight. I need to explain myself.'

A person wearing a white coat – a pharmacist – came into view and Walker moved aside to let her pass. After she'd gone through the door, he said, 'Okay. My place, Friday night. See you then.'

CHAPTER NINE

BY THE TIME Walker reached his office he felt exhausted. There was a stack of correspondence to go through and files had been dumped on his desk by the clerical staff with post-it notes demanding various chores. He pushed them aside and looked at his watch. It was only 11 am!

'I don't think I can do this anymore.' It was all too much – cancer patients, Marcia Links, Angela. He stared morosely at the stack of files. Maybe he could burn them. *I wonder if anyone would notice.* Maybe he could walk out with them under his arm and throw them in the boot of his car. No one would find them.

He leaned back in his chair and stared at the ceiling. What if he just left? Someone else would have to do his job. Who? He closed his eyes and let out a soft moan. It would end up being Angela, in the short term. The other oncologists were too busy and they wouldn't be able to get a replacement for months. 'I guess I'll have to stay,' he groaned. *But all I'm doing is looking after patients. Nothing else. Marcia Links can get stuffed. If anyone asks me to do just one more thing –*

The phone rang. He stared at it. On the fifth ring, he swore and flicked the receiver into his hand. 'What!' he barked.

'Kit. It's me.'

'What do you want, Wendy?' His voice was full of warning. He was in no mood for any more of Darling's guilt trips about Felicity. He made a fist. If he even mentioned her name ...

'That fellow we met the other night, Peter Runsack.'

'What of him?' he said through gritted teeth. Runsack had been talking about PNG, a little too close …

'He's dead.'

Walker said nothing for a moment as he stared at the wall before him. 'What?'

'His body was found in the harbour this morning. Walsh Bay.'

'Walsh Bay,' he said numbly. 'This morning? But I was there this morning.'

'You? What for?'

'Jogging.'

'Jogging! Since when do you jog?'

'How did he drown? What was he doing swimming there?'

'Not drowned. Strangled then thrown in. It was near the Sydney Theatre Company.'

'But I jogged past there.' He thought about what he'd seen. 'Those two girls who were in the pub, they were there. They were jogging out of the wharf when I went past.'

'You mean the dark-skinned woman and the blonde who were sitting near us at the Lord Nelson?'

'Yes.'

'I saw them too. They were coming into the Holiday Inn. I'd gone there to meet Runsack.'

'Do you think they could've killed him? Why them?'

'Probably not. But they might've seen something. I'll pass on the info and we can interview them.' Darling paused and when he spoke again he seemed hesitant. 'I saw Fred today at The Rocks Station.'

Walker flopped back in his chair, stunned. 'Fred Bowles. He's still there? What … what did you talk about?'

All he could think about was how he'd almost ended up in detention. It was Bowles who'd saved him. And he'd never thanked the policeman properly. He'd always meant to go back and talk to him but never had. There was no excuse; he lived only a short walk from the station. But he just didn't want to be reminded.

'I was asking him about the case,' said Darling. 'But he also mentioned you. And Felicity.'

Walker closed his eyes. Even Fred Bowles was talking about his wife. He should be furious but all the anger had drained from him.

Darling kept talking. 'He reckons I've been too rough on you.'

Walker said nothing.

Darling's voice was slow, uncertain. 'Maybe I have. I've given you a hard time about her. I've been a total dick. Fred reckons I should apologise.'

Walker remained silent, staring. He felt empty, like every emotion had been leached from his soul. He was too spent even to feel depressed. Depression took too much energy.

'So, I apologise,' said Darling.

He took a deep breath. 'Yep,' was all he could say before he gently placed the telephone receiver back onto its cradle. Soon after, he walked out of his office and headed for home.

Walker pulled up outside his terrace and turned the engine off, then immediately wished he hadn't. Standing near the front gate was a tall blonde dressed in a tight blue dress that hugged every curve of her body – Cassandra Hollow. Walker groaned, his hand poised to twist the key in the ignition, but he realised he couldn't run for long. She knew where he lived.

Cassandra used to be Darling's girlfriend. As far as Walker knew, Wendy probably thought she still was. But before his meltdown after Blinkton's death, Walker had started dating Cassandra. Or rather than dating, he'd been sleeping with her, since they didn't really do much else. Angela had rejected him that night in Epping Pub when he'd punched Craig Blinkton on the nose. He'd thought Angela had a thing for Blinkton but that theory had come unstuck when Blinkton kidnapped her and threatened to throw her off The Gap.

Walker had pushed Blinkton off the cliff. Or at least, he might have. It all happened so fast – the gun shot, Angela screaming, him jumping towards Blinkton. But he also remembered Angela's hand. He remembered she lashed out at Blinkton too. She could've pushed him.

'Are you okay, Chris?'

Cassandra's face was close to his, her forehead wrinkled with concern. She was leaning through the driver-side window. He could smell her perfume. Her full lips were so red.

'Eh!' he grunted. 'Sorry, I was daydreaming.'

She put her hand on his cheek. Soft and cool. 'I've been worried about you. You didn't answer the door when I came around. I didn't know where you were.'

'Sorry,' he mumbled. 'I haven't been myself.'

She smiled. 'You're here now. Are you okay?'

He nodded. 'Better.' He shifted, feeling uncomfortable being penned up in his car seat with her so close. She sensed his unease and pulled back. He smiled up at her. 'Do you want to go for a drink?'

'Love to.'

Five minutes later they were seated in a tiny side room at the Hero of Waterloo, Walker's local pub. A tall skinny barman with tousled hair and a large Adam's apple served them a beer and white wine, raising his eyebrows and giving a not-so-subtle wink at Walker as he glanced at Cassandra.

'Thank you, James,' said Cassandra, smiling up at him, her voice smooth, causing him to smile broadly in return.

'Nice to have you grace our four walls again, Cassie,' he said. 'This place can always do with a bit of class. Feel free to visit us anytime.' He nodded at Walker. 'With or without him.'

'Thanks, Jim,' Walker said meaningfully. He knew the barman hated that nickname. When he frowned his displeasure, Walker continued. 'Jimbo, I'm intrigued. I've been coming here all my life and I reckon you've barely said more than a handful of words to me on any one occasion. Why have you suddenly become so talkative?'

'Ah, Kit,' he nodded sagely. 'That is a very good question. Could it have something to do with the fact that you've barely said two words to me in all those years?'

Walker was stunned. 'Really? So you like to talk? I thought you were the silent brooding type.'

James indicated Cassandra with a nod of his head. 'Also helps to be easy on the eye, like our dear Cassie. Who is always pleasant and polite, I might add.' He smiled down at her and she reached out and patted his hand. 'You're usually a sloppy mess, if you don't mind me saying,' he added, addressing Walker. 'If you tidied yourself up a bit, the atmosphere might be more conducive.'

Stone-faced, Walker nodded but waved his hand for him to leave. 'Good to know, Jimmy. Good to know. Now you can bugger off.'

After James had left, Walker took a sip of his beer and gazed across the table. He had to admit, Cassandra was certainly one of the most beautiful women he'd ever seen. And for some reason, she liked him. She could have anyone she wanted (and often did, as far as he could determine) but right now, she wanted to be with him. According to her, she was serious about their relationship. She was also kind. She was clever. She was a defence lawyer. So why did he have doubts?

'You're too good for me.'

'What?'

Aghast, Walker realised he had spoken his thoughts.

'What?' he said dumbly.

Cassandra's face wore astonishment. 'You said that I'm too good for you.'

'Did I?'

'I'm not deaf.'

Walker took a big swig. He felt like a small animal in the spotlight of a hunting truck. 'Oh. Maybe I did then.'

'What do you mean?' She reached out and grabbed his hand. 'Chris, I'm not going to let you break up with me. That would be stupid. I refuse to let you make a bad decision because you're depressed.'

'Depressed?'

'Or whatever it is you have leftover from Felicity. You obviously haven't got over her. And I can understand that. You loved her dearly. You have lingering doubts over how she died. You're confused about it all. You can't sleep and you have nightmares over her.'

'How the hell did you know that?'

'Chris, we've spent many nights together. You talk in your sleep. You're deeply troubled. You can't get over her.'

'What?' How did she know so much?

'Something bad happened in New Guinea. And not just her drowning. There was something else. I can tell by your face in the morning after you've been dreaming. You have a look of … of horror. Dread. Or incomprehension maybe. Whatever happened, it's not resolved, at least not in your mind.'

Walker stared at her wordlessly. Did she know something? Maybe she'd found out. 'Do you know what happened?' he stuttered.

'No. But there is something terribly wrong. Something that Barry wouldn't talk about either.'

'Wendy?'

She let out an exasperated breath. 'Why do you call him that stupid name? It's childish.' She shook her head stiffly. 'Look, that doesn't matter. Call him what you want. The thing is, he's just as dark and brooding about Felicity as you are. And he's even worse since he came back from New Guinea. Won't even talk to me about it.'

'Have you been seeing him since we've been together? Have you been talking about me?'

'I haven't slept with him, if that's what you're asking. But I've spoken to him. I asked him what he found out about Felicity and he clammed up tighter than a choirgirl's legs.'

He didn't know what to say. Darling thought Walker had eaten his wife's flesh. Her brains. Just like the New Guinea natives used to do. Then the thing he didn't want to think about surged into his consciousness. He tried not to think about it but it buzzed around in his head, over and over.

Maybe he'd eaten the old man's brains. Maybe the old woman had fed them to him. Cassandra was a lawyer. She was smart but she wouldn't understand. That he might be infected with something awful. Worse than AIDS. A slow virus they called it, passed on to those who'd taken part in the funerary rites. An infection that rotted your brain. Kuru. Like mad cow disease. The virus could be destroying his brain now. In a few years, he could be a vegetable and then he'd die a demented, incontinent, dribbling, useless fool!

His hand jerked on the table. It began to feel numb. He was sure his lips were numb. He forced himself to look sideways. Was he seeing double again? He put his head in his hands and pushed his fingers through his hair. Kuru! He had it. He was sure of it. How long before everyone else could see it in him?

He raised his eyes to hers. 'Cassie, like I said, I'm no good. I've got something terrible wrong with me. I'm bad inside.'

'Nonsense,' she said. 'You're a good man.'

'Not like that.' He looked away. He couldn't meet her eyes. 'Not like that. I can't explain it.'

She reached out her hand. 'Come on, Chris. You need someone to look after you.' She gave a wide smile, soft and generous. 'Let me take you home.'

He jerked his hand away. 'No, I can't. Not now. I'm sorry Cassie but it's all too much. I'm no good for anyone.'

Her lips were tight. 'Okay, Chris, as you wish. I'll leave you alone. But not for long.' She reached out her hand again. 'I'm not going to lose you.'

CHAPTER TEN

WALKER GOT TO work earlier than usual after waking at six thinking about Cassandra. She liked him, he was sure, but although he wanted to feel the same towards her, he realised he just couldn't. She wanted more than a physical relationship and so did he, but not with her.

What do I see in Angela? he asked himself as he walked through the empty carpark. He didn't think she even liked him. Worse, he got the impression she felt sick whenever she saw him.

He heard footsteps and a shadow loomed towards him from the side, moving quickly. Walker raised his arms towards his attacker, letting out a short cry. The large figure stopped short and Walker stepped backwards.

'It's me,' hissed a voice.

Walker peered into the shadows. 'Ali? Is that you?'

'Yes, I just said it's me.' The large Lebanese bikie stepped into the light. He appeared to be wearing the exact same clothes as the other day. Walker quickly scanned the area looking for accomplices but saw no one.

'I want to thank you again for returning my grand-mère's locket,' Ali said in a low voice.

Walker thought he sounded menacing. Again, he looked around but there was no one.

'I said I owe you one,' continued Ali.

'There's no need —'

'I have some information about the man who came to your house that night.'

'Peter Runsack?' said Walker.

'I don't know his name. The man you met at the Lord Nelson. Big ears.' He flapped his hands beside his head. 'The man who was knocked off the next morning.'

'What of him? How do you now?' He had a sudden thought. 'Please don't tell me you killed him.'

'Me? No! I'm no murderer.' Ali dropped his voice. 'But I know some pretty rough people. Druggies, you know.'

'So?'

'Well, one of these druggies was at Walsh Bay the morning that man got killed.'

'Did he see anything?'

Ali looked around and moved closer. 'He was high at the time but he reckons he saw a bloke being strangled then chucked into the harbour. I didn't believe him at first, thought it was the drugs talking, but then I heard about the body being found. Too much of a coincidence. Then I saw the photo in the paper.'

'Did he see who did it?'

'White hair, real blond. Strong bastard, from what the druggie said.' Ali raised his hands to form a circle. 'Strangled him with his bare hands.'

Walker thought furiously. There had been a blond-haired fellow sitting near them that night in the Lord Nelson. 'Do you know the druggie's name? Will he talk to the police?'

Ali let out a short laugh. 'No way. Don't know his name and I don't know where to find him. But I know enough about him to say he won't talk to coppers. He's done enough time himself. He doesn't even know I'm telling you. He'd freak out if he knew, even though you're not a cop.'

'Did your druggie tell you anything else about the blond man?'

Ali tapped his finger above his lip. 'Silver stud in here.'

Walker thought back to the night at the pub but hadn't really taken that much notice of the people around them. He couldn't remember a silver stud. Maybe it wasn't him.

'Okay, thanks, Ali. I'll pass this on to the police.'

'Don't tell them I told you either. If I see a copper anywhere near me, I'll clam up. There'll be consequences and I won't be able to protect you.'

'If that's the case, the police probably won't believe me then.'

Ali raised his large hands. 'I've told you the info. You can do whatever you want. If you keep it to yourself then that's up to you.'

'Okay then.'

Ali kept his arms raised. 'So, are we even?'

'What?'

'For returning my locket?'

Walker shrugged. 'Sure. We're even.'

'Good. You won't see me again.'

Walker waved. 'Fine with me.'

Ali backed away then turned and walked away quickly.

Walker watched as he strode down the ramp into a large alcove full of tradies' vehicles where he hopped onto a large motorbike. The engine reverberated around the enclosed space, deafening Walker and causing him to wince until the bikie had driven away.

He sighed. *I guess I'll have to tell Wendy.*

Walker ambled towards his office, contemplating what Ali had told him. Why would Peter Runsack have been murdered? It had to have something to do with the circumstances around his brother's death. But why now? And who was the blond man? What did he have to do with it? And then there were the two young women he'd seen running from the wharf. What did they have to do with it?

Walker stopped stiffly in the corridor, concern creasing his forehead. It was all about New Guinea. That damn country was still torturing him. Felicity's death, him almost dying. Other awful, forgotten things. And now another murder linked with that terrible place. It was as if a demon had got hold of him in that wretched country and wanted to pull him back, never to be free, eternally suffering. He wanted nothing to do with it but now he had information, he'd have to share it with the police.

He began walking slowly again, deep in thought. Did he have to? What if he said nothing? Ali wouldn't tell anyone. He could keep it to himself. The cops would find out some other way, almost certainly. They had their ways.

He let out a deep breath. He knew he couldn't keep the secret. He had too many already. He didn't need another. He would have to tell Wendy.

Up ahead, walking away from him, was Holland Xavier, making his way to his own office. Walker's heart sank. He realised he'd have to talk to him about the claims of overtreatment made by Links the other day, apart from Peter Shore. She was over the top, that was certain, but he had to take notice of any complaints when it came to patient care, no matter how nutty they sounded. Then again, on more than one occasion he'd caught a whiff of alcohol on her breath. But even if she was an alcoholic, her accusations had to be handled properly. With a sigh, he realised he'd have to pass her door to get to his office. He desperately didn't want to have her ramming her objections down his throat, yet again.

He picked up speed as he approached Links' door and was relieved to see it was closed. He knew from experience that she tended to keep an eye on the corridor and had a habit of jumping out to harangue anyone passing about her latest crusade. He kept his head down as he walked along, not putting it past her to recognise people by their silhouette through the opaque glass in the door, or by the pattern of their footsteps. She might be a bit of a lunatic but she was also clever.

As he walked past, he was struck by a change in the air temperature, as if a heater had been turned on in the corridor. He kept moving, thinking that maybe Links had brought in a radiator from home or something equally preposterous. Then he slowed. That didn't make sense, even for Marcia Links. It was the end of summer. If anything, she'd have brought in a fan.

He walked back to the door. It felt warm. He touched the metal handle and jerked his hand away. It was hot! His mind raced. Fire! There must be a fire in the room!

He pulled his shirt sleeve down over his hand and tried the handle. Locked!

'Marcia!' he yelled. No response. He put his ear to the door. Still nothing. Walker looked up and down the long corridor. In the distance, he could see someone walking away but they were too far to help.

'Fire!' he yelled. No one came into the corridor. There was only one thing to do.

He stepped to the other side of the passage and rushed at the door, throwing his shoulder into it. The door refused to budge. It always looked so easy on TV. He raised his leg and kicked the door with the sole of his shoe. There was a crack. He kicked two more times then ran at the door with his shoulder again. It smashed open.

A conflagration rose from the office chair in front of the desk. Marcia Links was nowhere to be seen. Even as he watched, the high flames slowly dwindled to a simmering fire on what was left of the chair.

Then he saw it – a human leg at the base of the chair, still adorned with a high heel shoe. The type that Marcia liked to wear.

There was a strange odour in the air – the stench of burnt flesh but also another smell. Something that burned quickly. He couldn't place it but he'd smelled it before. He felt he should know it.

Then the flames were gone. Nothing else had burned. Just Marcia Links. Even the timber desk was merely singed. But then he saw the other thing. A ghastly skull with the skin and hair all burned away, sitting on its side on the chair remnant. And there was a human hand on the desk, unburnt, the arm gone. Between the fingers was a cigarette. It was as if the whole body had burned, magically leaving one lower leg, a skull and one hand.

Walker stumbled out into the corridor, which was now full of people. He saw one of the oncology secretaries. 'Please call security,' he gasped. 'And the police. No wait! I'll do that.' He'd call Darling himself. He'd know what to do.

Thirty minutes later, Walker was in his office with Darling and David Jones. The forensic team was swarming over Marcia Links' office and the corridor was abuzz with interested onlookers – ghouls, the cops called them – cordoned off by two burly policemen at two points in the corridor away from the scene.

Walker had finished telling his story, with both Darling and Jones jotting notes as he spoke and asking one or two questions. Walker knew the story sounded fanciful. He wouldn't believe it if someone told it to him. But the proof was in the pile of cinders and the half-burnt office chair with a skull and the two limb stumps. They asked him, more than once, if he was sure the door was locked; that maybe the timber was swollen from the fire and he only thought it was locked; that he was excited and hadn't turned the handle properly.

'Wendy,' Walker said with some exasperation when Darling asked him once again. 'I've been to umpteen cardiac arrests and seen all sorts of human tragedy and ghastly injuries in my time. You just have to believe me when I say I wasn't over-excited. My head was level. The door *was* locked.'

'Okay, okay,' said Darling. 'In fact, I've checked the lock on the door. It was locked.'

Walker threw up his hands. 'So why pester me?'

'We have to make sure. Just one more question. Did you lock the door after you entered?'

He threw his head back in frustration then leaned close to Darling's face. 'No. I. Did. Not.'

Darling merely grunted and scribbled something on his pad.

Jocelyn Banks, the forensic pathologist, came into Walker's office – neat auburn hair, pearl earrings and a manner that brooked no argument. She rolled a set of surgical gloves off her hands and threw them neatly into the bin then patted a delicate hand over her hair. 'Well, boys, I don't know how you do it but you continue to surprise me – and that's saying something. I thought I'd seen everything.'

Walker believed her. Banks was the chief pathologist for the forensic morgue of Western Sydney and had been involved with untold number of grisly murders of all descriptions.

'I think this might be a case of spontaneous combustion. Can you believe it?'

Jones screwed his face up. 'Spontaneous combustion? What's that?'

'It's where someone spontaneously combusts,' Jocelyn told the young officer, her eyebrows raised. She continued when it was clear that Jones did not understand. 'The body explodes into flames for no obvious cause.'

'You're kidding,' said Walker.

'Is that a real thing?' added Darling, his face showing disbelief.

'Yes, it is a real thing,' said Jocelyn. Then she gave an uncertain look. 'Well, maybe it's real. There are several cases in the medical literature. The description is classic. An incinerated body with nothing else around it much damaged, leaving a skull and unburnt limbs. But I must say, I've always doubted the validity of the phenomenon.'

'But you think this could be it?' said Walker. 'There's no obvious cause. The door was locked.'

Jocelyn shrugged. 'I suggest we exclude every other possibility before we call it that. I don't want to be a laughing-stock.'

'What else could it be?' asked Jones.

With a look of irritation, Jocelyn said, 'I don't know, constable, you're the policeman. You figure it out.'

'She'd been smoking,' Jones said earnestly. 'I would hardly call that no obvious cause for a fire.'

'There is that,' Jocelyn conceded with a nod.

'There was a pack of these in her top drawer.' Jones held up a clear plastic bag that contained a packet of Marlboros. 'Smoking Causes Lung Cancer' was printed in bold upper case in the middle of the distinctive red flip-top.

'At least she didn't die of lung cancer,' said Walker, drawing a look from Jocelyn.

'There was also a disposable cigarette lighter on the desk,' added Jones.

'Hardly a good reason for her to catch on fire,' said Walker. 'If that was all you needed, we'd have people bursting into flames all over the western suburbs. They smoke like chimneys out here.'

'Typically, spontaneous combustion has been described in elderly people who are heavy drinkers,' said Jocelyn. She addressed Walker. 'Do you know her well enough to describe her habits?'

'I don't like to tell tales …'

'Come on, Kit,' snapped Darling. 'This is a murder investigation.'

'Okay, Wendy,' he replied with equal heat. 'Don't play the superior cop with me, otherwise I won't help you at all.'

'You're not doing me any favours, Kit,' said Darling. 'You're obliged to tell me anything you know, otherwise you could be had for obstruction of justice.'

'So, you going to arrest me now, are you, Wendy?'

'Just tell me what you know,' growled Darling. 'Stop playing silly buggers.'

Walker paused to gather his thoughts. 'Okay, I'm sorry, Wendy. It's just this has shaken me up a bit. Of course I will help.' He continued more slowly. 'I'm pretty sure I've smelled alcohol on her breath on more than one occasion lately.'

'Pretty sure?' said Darling.

Walker screwed up his mouth. 'Well, I wasn't in the habit of getting physically close to her. If you must know, I found her quite obnoxious.' He scratched his chin. 'But, yes, I'm sure I could smell alcohol. And another thing – when I came into her office … when she was burning … I thought I could smell something.'

'Like what?' demanded Darling.

'Something sweet. Like sweet alcohol.' Walker shut his eyes, trying to recall. Then he opened them. 'Like Drambuie, or something like that. Sweet and alcoholic.'

'Drambuie,' said Jones, sounding impressed. 'Expensive.'

'What's cost got to do with it, Jones?' Darling berated.

'Just saying that Drambuie sounds expensive,' Jones replied defensively.

Darling shook his head and continued to frown at Jones as he spoke to Walker and Jocelyn. 'I think we have probably gone as far as we can sensibly go today.' His eyes shifted to the pathologist. 'I'll leave you to finish your autopsy, Dr Banks. Please let me know if you find anything that could suggest a cause of death other than spontaneous combustion. For the moment, I'll just record the death as suspicious, pending further investigation. Like you, I don't want to be made a laughing-stock either.'

After Jocelyn had left, Walker remained behind, examining the various pieces of burnt furniture while Jones looked on sternly.

'Something else on your mind, Kit?' asked Darling. 'Shouldn't you be getting back to work?'

'There is something else,' he said, glancing at Jones. 'But not about this.'

'About what then?'

'About the Lord Nelson the other night and our Lebanese friend.'

Darling turned to Jones. 'Leave us for a sec. This is about another case.'

After he'd left, Walker told Darling about his meeting with Ali Harb, and the unnamed druggie who had witnessed the murder.

'White-haired, you say. There was a white-haired fellow in the pub. And I saw him the next morning as I was going out of the Holiday Inn. South African by his accent.'

'What about the two girls?'

'They were also staying at the Holiday Inn. Australian, according to the desk clerk. Checked in the same day as the Runsack and checked out the morning of the murder. They had booked for two more days but told the desk staff that something had come up and they had to leave. The clerk thought one girl was Aboriginal.'

'What are you going to do?'

'Report it, of course. To Fred Bowles. It's not my case.'

'Okay,' said Walker, turning to leave. 'Just glad to have it off my chest. I'll leave it to you.'

'I meant what I said the other day,' blurted Darling.

Walker turned back, pretending not to understand.

Darling continued more slowly. 'About being too hard on you. You'd lost Felicity and all I could do was blame you. That was wrong.'

He dropped his head and turned to leave again. But as he reached the door he turned back. 'Well, that's the thing, Wendy. Maybe you're not wrong. Maybe you can forgive me but I can't forgive myself. I know something happened the day Felicity died, something more than I can remember. And afterwards. In the hut. Things that maybe I've blocked out. But until I know the truth – good or bad – I'll never rest.'

CHAPTER ELEVEN

DARLING PLACED THE phone receiver on the cradle and leaned back in his chair with a reflective look on his face.

'What did she say?' asked Jones, sitting at a nearby desk.

'Still says spontaneous combustion.' He frowned and pushed out his cheeks. 'Although I can sense she's hesitant. Says she wants to wait till the inquest. But so far, that's all she can come up with. Banks says it's a classic description. The door was locked from the inside. There's no other obvious cause.'

Jones scratched his head. 'But how can a person just burst into flames?'

Darling stood up. 'I don't know, Jones. I'm a policeman, not a scientist.' He squinted out onto the Parramatta streets. 'And we've come up with nothing either, so I guess we'll just have to accept it. Doesn't sit right though.'

'What about Dr Xavier? We have several witnesses saying there was tension between them. She vowed to go to administration to complain about the standard of his patient care.'

'There is that,' said Darling, nodding. 'But how did he kill her?'

Jones shrugged. 'Good motive though.' His face brightened. 'Maybe he had some clever chemical that bursts into flames by itself. He's a doctor. He could've got something from a lab or something.'

Darling pursed his lips in thought. 'There was that odour that Kit mentioned.'

'Drambuie?'

'*Like* Drambuie,' he said. 'I doubt the good doctor would've thrown a bottle of expensive liqueur on Links, expecting her to later burst into flames.'

'Could Links have been drinking Drambuie, spilled it, and then caught on fire from her cigarette?'

'Where's the empty bottle? It would need to have been the whole bottle. She'd have to shower in it.'

Jones gave a disheartened sigh. 'We checked the showers up the corridor. No alcohol bottles.'

Darling screwed up his face. 'I was only j –' He shook his head. 'Doesn't matter.'

Jones threw his head back in thought. 'Maybe she used another shower. There are some downstairs from her office near the morgue.'

'Yes,' Darling said sarcastically. 'You sound like you're onto something there, Sherlock.'

He jumped to his feet. 'Sir, I would like permission to go out and buy a bottle of Drambuie, so we can run a few tests.'

'What?'

'We could soak some cloth in the alcohol and see how readily it catches fire with a cigarette.'

'Are you serious?'

Jones had the look of an excited teenager. 'It might be the breakthrough we're after.'

Darling let out a short laugh. 'Sure, Jones. Your enthusiasm is impressive, if not your logic.'

'Sir,' he continued earnestly. 'Do I have permission to buy a large bottle?'

'The largest you can find,' Darling said expansively. 'Come to think of it, buy two while you're at it. I have an idea of what we can do with any leftovers.'

'Righto, sir.' He made for the door. 'I'll be back in a jiffy.'

Darling held up a hand. 'Steady on, Jones, I was only pulling your leg. Regardless of what Dr Banks said, we need to treat this like a normal case. As interesting as spontaneous combustion sounds, we have to consider more likely scenarios.'

'Like?'

'Murder of course.'

'But who?'

'That's our job, Jones. Murderers aren't always going to stand out like dogs' balls. You've already mentioned Dr Xavier. And there are the reports of a disagreement between Links and one of her patients.' He looked at his notebook. 'Mr Peter Shore. And there's a son, Jason Shore, who was involved with the same disagreement.'

'What was it about?'

Darling flipped his notebook closed. 'That's what we have to find out. I suggest we interview all three. And I want to talk to Dr Walker again.'

They met up with Walker in his office. His desk was strewn with paperwork and the in-tray was piled high with letters and notes. On the wall was a poster showing a picture of a cell with a double-helix and lots of scientific names and arrows.

'I want to find out more about the morning Marcia Links died,' said Darling.

'I've told you everything I know.' He shrugged. 'Happy to go over it again, though, if you think it will help.'

'I want to ask you about just before you found her.'

Walker leaned back in his chair. 'Okay,' he said slowly.

'Where did you come from?'

He stared at the ceiling in thought before he replied. 'I'd just parked my car. I had just had that … encounter,' he glanced at Jones then back to Darling, 'with our Lebanese friend.'

'Okay. Now I want you to think carefully. Did you see anyone just before you reached Marcia's office? Anyone coming away.'

'Lots of people in the main hospital corridor, of course.' He frowned. 'But no one in the clinical sciences corridor.' He shook his head. 'No, no one.' Then he raised his finger. 'Wait. Yes, Holland was walking into his office.'

'Dr Holland Xavier? Where is his office in relation to Dr Links'?'

'About five doors up. On the other side of the secretaries.'

'Was he walking away or to Dr Links office?'

Walker frowned. 'Away, I think.'

Darling jotted a note. 'Good.'

'Good?'

'Good that you can remember.'

'Hang on, Wendy, you don't think Holland would go as far as to murder Marcia?'

'At this stage, we don't think anything, Kit. We are merely gathering facts.'

'Well, I don't think he'd do that.'

'I'll note that. But we need to gather all the information.'

'You didn't note it,' said Walker.

'What?'

'You jot everything down but you didn't write that I don't think Holland is capable of murder.'

Darling smiled. 'We're all capable of murder, Kit. In the right circumstances.' He resisted the temptation of saying, 'Even you.'

Walker shifted uneasily.

'Is there anything else you can think of?' continued Darling. 'Anybody else in the vicinity? Anything you think was in her office that was out of place? Or anything missing?'

Walker shook his head slowly. 'No, not that I can think of.' He raised his finger. 'What about the fish?'

'Fish?'

'Marcia had this gold fish necklace. Given to her by Kubler-Ross. A giant in the palliative care world,' he explained after Darling raised an eyebrow. 'I've never seen her without it.'

'Probably melted,' said Jones.

'But you would have found evidence of it,' said Walker. 'Gold doesn't vaporise.'

Darling made a note. 'We'll look into it.'

An hour later, they were on the cancer ward at the hospital, having gained permission from the nurse manager to interview Peter Shore. The patient was in bed with the covers up to his chin, his face pale, his eyes closed. They introduced themselves to his son, Jason, who sat at the bedside with a portable computer open on the bedstand, which had been set up like a desk. He was reading a pamphlet, which he placed on the table when they entered.

'I'm afraid Dad's taken a turn for the worse. The chemo seems to be catching up with him.'

'We'll only be a moment,' Darling said. 'As you may have heard, Dr Marcia Links died the other day.' When the son nodded, he continued. 'We understand that there was a disagreement about your father's care the day before she died.'

The patient opened his eyes. 'It was nothing.' His voice was weak. 'She wanted to offer me palliative care. I insisted on having the chemo. Maybe I should have listened to her. Now I'm as crook as Rookwood.'

'According to one of the nurses, the conversation got pretty heated.'

'We disagreed, yes. I wouldn't say heated.' The patient let out a weak laugh. 'You think I might have killed her over it?'

'What about you, Jason?' Darling continued. 'I understand you had words with Dr Links.' He glanced at his notes. 'Called you stupid and selfish.' He looked up. 'Strong words from a doctor. Would have made me quite angry.'

'I can assure you, I took no offence. I'm sure she thought she was doing her job.'

'She threatened to go to administration and stop your father getting the chemotherapy he wanted.'

'Well, obviously that had no effect.' He waved his hand at his father, who had closed his eyes again. 'He got what he wanted.'

'Although I'm led to believe she never spoke to administration. Couldn't do; she was dead.'

'I'm sure she just changed her mind,' said Jason.

Darling was silent as he studied Jason's face. 'Where were you on the morning that Dr Links died?'

'What day was that?'

'Tuesday.'

Jason appeared to think for a moment. 'Same as every morning. I was here at my father's bedside.'

'For the whole morning?'

'Yes, the whole morning. I usually leave at about 1 pm. Work is very understanding.'

'What do you do?'

'I'm a printer.'

Darling pointed at the pamphlet that Jason had been reading and which was now on the table. 'That sort of thing? Do you mind?' he added as he picked it up. He had the impression that Jason was unhappy with him doing so.

It was single piece of paper. On one side it said, 'Learn to fly – Macquarie Model Airplane Club. Open day this Sunday'. He turned it over to see a colour photo of happy people gathered around a collection of brightly painted model airplanes. 'Model planes, eh? Nice.'

Jason was frowning. 'That's a freebie. I've done the design and printing for free. I'm a member.' He grasped the paper and tugged it out of Darling's hand. 'Do you mind? I'm proofreading it. It's the only copy.'

Darling indicated to Jones to continue the questions.

Jones obliged. 'You say you didn't leave. Not even for coffee?'

Jason hesitated. 'I usually get one. I probably did, although I can't be sure.'

'What time do you go for coffee?'

'If I have it?'

'If you have one.'

Jason grimaced in thought. 'About eleven, I guess.'

'Seems late for coffee,' said Jones.

'That's what time I have it.'

'Where do you get it?' Jones continued.

'There's only one coffee shop. The one in the foyer.'

Jones scribbled in his notepad then glanced at Darling, who shook his head subtly.

'That's it then,' said Jones. 'Please make sure you stay in Sydney. We may need to question you again.'

Jason indicated his father. 'Can't see me going anywhere, can you?'

After they had left the room, Darling said to Jones, 'Check his story. Question the nurses about the time and check with the coffee shop.'

'What about you?'

'I'm going to check something else out. This Sunday.'

CHAPTER TWELVE

ANGELA ARRIVED AT six when the sun was still a hand-span above Balmain. Walker had been nervously pacing the front room, checking himself in the mirror above the mantel, when he'd seen her pull up in her Accord. He'd watched her approach, standing beside the window just out of sight. She was dressed in jeans and a plain top, no jewellery or makeup. Definitely not dressed to impress. She had a simple beauty about her, with her slim build, shining dark hair pulled back in a red scrunchy and smooth tan skin. She was also clever and had a caring side, although he'd witnessed it more often with her patients than with him.

He felt a jab of pain in his jaw and he realised he'd been biting down. He wasn't sure what she had to say but it would either be abhorrence about him possibly ingesting his wife's dead body, or loathing because he'd let her down. Or fury and disillusion because she'd found that he was sleeping with Cassie. Whatever her emotions, he knew he deserved them all. He decided he'd just have to cop it sweet.

Walker answered the knock and led her into the front room then stood at the mantel. She seemed ill at ease and looked around the room as if it was her first time there, before eventually sitting down on the only lounge, her hands clasped together on her knees. Walker remained standing.

'It was terrible news about Dr Links,' she said, failing to meet his gaze.

'Yes, terrible.' He was sure she hadn't come to talk about Marcia Links' death. He waited.

Finally, she looked up at him with dark eyes. 'Chris, I feel that I have to explain myself.'

He was taken aback. 'You? Explain? Explain what?' If anything, he should be explaining his actions to her.

'Why I've been acting like this.'

He lowered himself beside her. 'Acting like what?'

She looked away. 'Distant. Empty.'

Walker had to admit, she'd been both of those things. But he thought it was because of the things he'd done, or might have done – things he couldn't even be sure of. 'Okay,' he said. 'I'm listening.'

'I said that we had to trust each other. And I know you tried. But after Craig Blinkton … and then after what Barry said you'd done …' She swallowed. 'Eaten her …' She pursed her lips as if she felt sick. 'Things came unstuck.' She closed her eyes tight shut as if she was in pain. 'I can't help myself.'

'What do you mean?' What was she talking about?

'Don't you remember? At the pub that night … You and me … I lusted after you! I wanted to sleep with you. I would've let you do anything to me!' Finally, she looked at him, her eyes full of tears. 'I must fight against it.' She let out a sob and put her face in her hands.

Walker raised his hand to comfort her but she pulled away.

She was crying. 'I've told you before. My mother's lust destroyed her. I know what my father did was wrong but she should've resisted. I don't want to be like that. I want to be in control. And it's my reluctance to get physical with you that's driven you away, made you sleep with Cassie.' She rubbed her eyes. 'Which is why we can't see each other. Not until I'm better.'

'Better?' Walker was dumbfounded. 'What do you mean?'

'I need to overcome this lust I have. I need to learn to control myself. I'll be seeking professional help.' She stood up stiffly and finally met his eyes. 'Please don't ask me out again. Please don't be nice to me at work. We must work together but we need to keep it professional. Superficial.'

Without waiting for his reply, she was gone, walking quickly out the front door and closing it behind her. A moment later, Walker heard her car start and speed off.

He sat back in the chair and let out a breath. Could it be true? She'd said the same before but then she went out to the pub with him, so he assumed she'd got over it.

He realised he was grinding his teeth again and he forced his mouth open. What she said didn't seem right. No one could be that screwed up about sex. He just didn't believe it. Her 'lust', as she described it, was just normal, as far as he was concerned. She was pushing him away. Giving him an excuse to sleep with Cassandra. There could only be one explanation.

She doesn't like me. And she's seeing someone else. She's just too chicken to tell me to my face.

Barry Darling met Sally Biggs outside of her lodgings on Glebe Point Road on Saturday morning and together they walked down the hill to Bridge Road. There was an open house at one of the properties for sale and Darling was interested. He'd saved enough for a deposit and had the go-ahead from the Police Credit Union, after the necessary checks and providing it was less than two hundred thousand. Darling thought he was in with a chance.

'Thanks for coming,' he said to Sally as she walked companionably by his side, their arms occasionally touching.

She pulled her straw-blond fringe away from her eyes to show a fresh, freckled face. 'No worries, Barry. It's exciting. I've never known anyone who could actually buy a house in Sydney. Everyone I know rents.'

He squinted up into the bright blue sky. It was a pleasant twenty-seven degrees with a soft breeze blowing. 'Nice day for the beach. You could've done that.'

'I thought you wanted me to come?'

Darling raised his hands. 'No, no. I love that you've come. I just don't want to impose.'

Sally looked at him from the corner of her eye and gave a cheeky smile. 'Okay then, if you want to be like that, you can owe me one. Happy?'

'Sure,' he said. 'A coffee?'

'Maybe. Maybe something better than that.'

Darling continued down Bridge Road wearing a slight frown, unsure of what she meant. They reached the property, a two-storey terrace in a row of about six. On the footpath was a sign that read 'L J Hooker Open House', with an arrow pointing to the house. It was a narrow, single-fronted terrace close to the footpath, with a small garden and front steps going up to an open front door, painted red. At the door stood a chunky fellow with dark hair and a tight suit, who grinned them a welcome.

'Looks nice,' said Sally, staring up at the terrace. It had a small veranda on the second floor with a brightly painted cast-iron balustrade.

'Small,' said Darling, trying not to feel too excited. It looked to be exactly what he wanted but he didn't want to appear eager to the real estate agent.

The agent looked Italian and introduced himself as Stan Cosmo. Except for the fact that he was a bit overweight, Darling was struck by how much the agent looked like him. A lot of people told Darling that he looked Mediterranean and he always met the suggestion with ambivalence.

'I'm the principal agent,' said Stan after Darling introduced himself. 'And this would be your lovely wife?'

Sally burst out laughing.

'No,' said Darling, embarrassed. 'A good friend.'

Sally grabbed his arm, still beaming, and introduced herself as they moved into the house. The terrace was tiny with a lounge room at the front, a small bathroom in the middle and a kitchen out back that led onto a neat courtyard. Upstairs was the main bedroom and then another set of narrow stairs led to an attic with another small bedroom. The main bedroom had double French doors that led out onto a veranda, the sound of passing cars clearly audible. But the house was clean and freshly painted and well-lit, and overall gave a pleasant feeling.

Darling checked the water pressure and flicked a few light switches. 'Everything seems to be in working order,' he said officiously, trying to give the impression he did this sort of thing on a regular basis.

'Lovely little package,' Stan said when they met again in the front room. 'Perfect for one …' he glanced at Sally, 'or two people. Maybe not if you're thinking of kids but it's perfect for a couple.'

Sally giggled again. She hadn't stopped smiling since they'd entered the house but had kept her opinions to herself.

'Mmm,' said Darling, trying to show he was not particularly taken with the place. He looked around at the ceilings and screwed his face up with mild distaste. 'What are they asking for it?'

'One ninety-five,' said Stan. 'But I'm sure the vendors will respond to a sensible offer. They've put a deposit on another place in Balmain and are looking for a quick settlement.'

Darling gave another murmur, stroked his chin and adopted a slight frown. 'A quick settlement. It might be hard to find a buyer who's ready.'

'This could be a great chance for someone looking to get into the market,' said Stan. 'The market's paused but who knows how long before it takes off again. Look at the gains in the last five years. The Sydney property market is the place to be. Get in early and you could make yourself a tidy profit.'

Darling nodded sagely, trying not to appear nervous. The market taking off again was the thing that worried him the most. He could afford a house now – just – but if things got more expensive again, he'd be left behind. He extended his hand to Stan. 'Well, thanks for showing us around. We have a few other properties to look at. We'll definitely think about it.'

'By all means,' said Stan. 'Have a think about it. You two have a talk.' He gave Darling a business card. 'Give me a call this afternoon if you want. As I said, happy to consider offers.'

As they were leaving, two other couples were coming through the front door and they had to stand aside to let them through. Both looked like professional couples, causing Darling's heart to sink.

He scowled when he reached the footpath. 'Yuppies,' he murmured. 'How can I compete with them?'

Sally grabbed his upper arm and pulled him close. She was still smiling. 'That was fun! Where are these other properties *we* must look at? I loved the way you told Stan that *we* would have to think about it.'

Darling was about to put her straight when he checked himself. It felt right to have Sally holding his arm. And it felt right looking at houses with her. She seemed to sense his thoughts since she leaned in and gave him a long kiss on his cheek. He finally broke into a great smile. He felt happy. He felt confident. He could afford this house. He could even afford their asking price without putting in an offer.

He twisted his head to catch Sally's eyes. 'Do you really like it? I do. I think I'll put in an offer.' He patted her hand and pulled her close. 'Come on, let's get this cup of coffee I owe you and we'll talk it over.'

CHAPTER THIRTEEN

DARLING TURNED HIS Commodore off Epping Road and wound his way through the backstreets of Marsfield until he found the university sports fields, tucked amid thick bushland some way from the university campus. The area had multiple playing fields and Darling wondered at the massive land area the university owned.

Sally also seemed impressed. 'What do they study here?' she asked, her voice touched with awe. He'd asked Sally to accompany him and he was pleased she had jumped at the suggestion.

He grimaced. 'Nothing much, apparently. Club Mac, they call it. More like a resort than a uni. I think they teach business management and childcare, stuff like that.'

'Medicine?'

'I don't think so. It's pretty soft-core.'

'It would be lovely to study here. The grounds are so beautiful.'

The high-pitched buzz of model engines greeted them as they entered the complex and Darling turned into the carpark of the first grounds on the right, the sign as they entered declaring it to be Roger Sheeran Oval. They watched the model planes flit over the field for a few minutes before getting out of the car. Most were control-line models with the pilot standing in the park, guiding the plane using lines attached to it. But further away Darling could see models flying without any apparent connection.

'Wow,' he remarked, pointing at them. 'They must be radio-controlled.' Nearer to them, a small crowd of people, mostly men, were grouped together on the grass outside the clubhouse, surrounded by model planes of all sizes and description. The air smelled of burnt fuel and oil.

Darling identified a Spitfire and a Sopwith Camel biplane but there were many other varieties that he couldn't name. A red triplane, which he guessed was a Fokker, was taxiing away as they approached and they stopped to watch as the craft lifted smoothly off the grass, its little engine screaming. The red plane ascended quickly before its controller threw the craft into a dive towards the ground, pulling out with only a few metres to spare. Darling glanced at Sally and was pleased to see she had a huge smile on her face.

Nearby, a fellow was preparing a racy blue mono-winged number that looked like one of the stunt planes the US Airforce flew and Darling and Sally moved for a closer look. It was a line-controlled model with fine stainless-steel guide wires running through an eye in the wing into the fuselage. The fellow was gangly with wispy hair and looked little more than a teenager, but he smiled confidently as they approached and seemed more than happy for them to look on as he went about his business.

'Looks fast,' commented Sally.

The fellow, who was on his knees next to the plane, smiled up at her. 'It is. Club champion.'

Sally gave an impressed murmur. Darling moved closer. 'What sort of engine is it, if you don't mind me asking?'

'Not at all. It's an ASP 2-Stroke Nitro Glow. It's a little beauty. 1.75 horse-power at 17,000 revs. A bit over-powered, if anything. But it goes like the clappers.' As he spoke, he connected a flexible tube to a nipple on the side of the engine cowling. The plastic tube led to a plastic canister which the fellow squeezed, pushing fuel into the tank.

'What type of fuel do you use?' asked Sally.

Again, the man smiled. 'Trade secret. The exact formula, that is. But it's glow fuel – a mixture of methanol, castor oil and a bit of nitro.' He squeezed some of the liquid into a small container. He took a sniff then handed it to Sally. 'Get a whiff of that. I love the smell."

Sally bent her head over the beaker and breathed in carefully then handed it to Darling who cautiously did the same. It smelled of speed and power. He sensed the gas vaporising in the air as he breathed it in, leaving a sweet odour in his nostrils. Then he gazed out at the field beyond in thought.

'Not Drambuie …' he murmured. He turned to Sally. 'At the hospital,' he said. 'Marcia Links.'

'You had a friend burnt by this stuff?' said the fellow. 'Easy enough to do. It's so flammable. You gotta be so careful. Is your friend a member of the club? I don't recognise the name.'

Darling shook his head. 'What about another name? Jason Shore?'

'Jason? Yes, he's a member.' He looked around at the crowd. 'Haven't seen him for a while though. I think his father's sick.'

Darling nodded. 'Thanks. Thank you very much.' He grabbed Sally's hand. 'That's all I need to know.'

CHAPTER FOURTEEN

ON MONDAY MORNING, Walker arrived at the outpatient clinic with a rising dread. He didn't want to see Angela and he didn't want to see cancer patients. Both had too many problems. He had enough of his own. He paused in the waiting area and looked along the corridor – lime-green doors and brown carpet. The sight of them made him feel sick. He wondered how the patients felt about it. With a sigh, he entered the clinic area that held all the patient files. Two nurses were going through the stack. Angela was waiting for him.

'We have a new patient,' said Angela, without greeting him. She sounded very professional. 'Mrs Betty Boyce, aged sixty-two. Sent along by the GP for investigation of anaemia.'

So, is this what it is going to be like? Distant. Cold.

'To us?' he asked. He didn't really feel like being here. 'Why us? Why not haematology?'

'She's already seen them. And gastroenterology.'

Walker folded his arms. 'Again, why us?'

'Well, she has a history of kidney cancer resected three years ago and I guess the GP is clutching at straws.'

Walker's interest was twigged. 'Go on.'

Angela consulted her notes. 'As I said, clear cell renal carcinoma removed by nephrectomy three years ago. It was twenty centimetres, grade 4, one lymph node positive but all completely resected, no known metastases. She's otherwise well. A bit of hypertension treated with beta-blockers. No family history. Found to be anaemic about a month ago on a blood test by the GP.' Angela looked up. 'She was feeling a bit lethargic.' She referred to her notes again. 'Haematology confirms iron deficiency anaemia. Serum ferritin is low and red cells are microcytic, all consistent with blood loss.' Angela looked up again. 'No obvious source. Haematology referred her to gastroenterology and they performed an upper and lower endoscopy, which were both clear.'

'Who did the scope?' asked Walker. Angela mentioned the name of one of the hospital's best gastroenterologists and he grunted, satisfied that a lesion was unlikely to have been missed. 'So, she must be bleeding from the small bowel then.'

'Yes. But I'm not sure why the GP referred her to us.'

Walker rubbed his chin. 'That was a pretty big tumour. And there was cancer in one of the resected nodes so a high chance of recurrence.'

'Nothing shows on the CT of the chest, abdomen and pelvis.'

'Let's look at it to double-check.'

Angela placed the films on the viewing box and Walker went through them carefully, paying particular attention to the small bowel. 'Duodenum looks normal. How far did they get the scope down?'

Angela flicked to a report in the file. 'To the first part of duodenum. They couldn't get the scope further.'

'Fair enough. Is the gastro team planning anything else?'

'A barium swallow and follow-through. She's having it next week.'

Walker nodded. 'Good.' He turned to Angela. 'What do you think she'll have?'

Angela tipped her head to the side. 'Why do I sense a bet coming on?'

'Ah, so you want to bet?' He was glad they could still banter on a professional level. At least he didn't have to practise in an environment of uncomfortable animosity.

'I didn't say that. But I know what you're like when you get that smarty-pants attitude. You think you know what it is and you're trying to show off.'

Walker looked indignant. 'Smarty-pants. I'm not a smarty-pants.'

'Sometimes you are. You're a full-on smarty-pants when you think you're right about something obscure.'

He shrugged his shoulders. 'Okay, clever dick, what do you think it is then?'

'By the way you're making a big deal out of it, I'd say it's likely to be metastatic kidney cancer to the small bowel.' She gave a haughty look.

'What makes you say that?' He felt a bit deflated. 'That would be very unusual.'

'Not for renal cell cancer. It can spread almost anywhere and often it's an isolated recurrence.'

'Looks like someone has been doing her reading.'

'I'm in training, Dr Walker. I think I'm supposed to be reading.'

He noted how she called him doctor and not Chris. 'Fair enough. If that's what it is, how should it be treated?'

Now she became less certain and paused in thought. 'Interleukin-2? But that's pretty toxic.'

He nodded. 'Anything else?'

Angela gave a blank look.

'There's also interferon,' he continued. 'But that's even less effective than interleukin. Anyway, I don't think she needs drugs.'

'Okay, what should we do?'

By now, Walker had regained his usual confidence. 'Let's go and see Mrs Boyce and discuss it with her.'

Betty Boyce was a short, plump sixty-year-old with grey hair cut short, wearing tracksuit bottoms, runners and a large T-shirt that had 'Cheeky Grandma' printed on the chest. She was talkative and seemed happy to go through the story again with Walker, even without his encouragement.

'It all started a few months ago when I became really tired. Not sleepy, you know, but exhausted. I could hardly get myself up the front steps into my house. So I went to my GP and he first told me it was probably a virus and not to worry. But it didn't get better so I marched back in to see him and demanded a blood test, see. And that showed –'

Walker interrupted. 'Thanks, Mrs Boyce. Dr Chee has already told me the full story. We find it fascinating.'

'Really?' She seemed pleased. 'I'm glad I'm a medical curiosity. No one seems to be able to work out what's wrong. I've had one of those tubes shoved up my –'

'Yes,' interrupted Walker again smoothly. 'We have all the test results.'

'So, what do you think is wrong?' Betty grinned. 'Maybe they'll have to open me up and have a look inside?'

Walker nodded. 'Yes, I think we will.'

Her face dropped. 'Eh?'

'Yes, we might have to operate.'

'Operate? Operate on what? Do you mean open me up again like the kidney operation? That was huge.'

'Not exactly. But I think it will be a big operation. We think you're bleeding from the small bowel.'

'They're doing a barium thing next week. And the other fellow says that if that's normal he wants to do another test. Squirt dye into my blood vessels.'

'An angiogram?' Walker threw Angela a questioning look but she shook her head. She'd obviously missed that information.

He turned back to the patient. 'They must be thinking of a bleeding blood vessel. We call it an AV malformation.'

'Sounds bad.'

'But I doubt it's that. I think it's probably the kidney cancer that's come back in the small bowel.'

'But the surgeon said he'd got it all. Why would I have bowel cancer?'

'Not bowel cancer,' corrected Angela. 'The kidney cancer may have spread to the bowel before the kidney was removed. It's taken this long to show up.'

'Oh?' said Betty, although her blank face hinted she didn't understand. 'But he said he got it all.'

'All he could see,' added Angela. 'Sometimes the cancer cells are so small, you don't know they're there until later when they grow enough to cause problems.'

'Like bleeding?'

'Yes, like bleeding.'

Mrs Boyce sat quietly for a few moments as she struggled to assimilate the news.

Finally, Walker put his hand on her arm. 'But we don't know for sure, Betty. Let's see what the next tests show. Can you come back and see us in a couple of weeks?'

Betty nodded. Angela held her hand. 'Is there someone who can come with you next time? It's a lot that we're telling you. It would be good to have a friend or relative.'

Again she nodded, still appearing stunned. 'Yes. Yes, I'll ask my sister.'

Later, when they'd finished the clinic and the nurses had wandered off to other duties, Walker waited until Angela finished with her notes. She seemed to sense him waiting and he noticed her movements became stilted, and she purposefully refused to look at him, keeping her head buried in the files.

Finally, he couldn't wait. 'Angela, I think we need to talk.'

She slapped the file closed and turned to him. 'No, we don't,' she said firmly. 'I've said all I want to say. It won't help to talk any more about it. It's my problem to deal with. You can't do anything about it. I was hoping you'd keep your end of the deal. We can't have personal chitchat while we're at work.'

'Deal? I made no deal. You just made your ridiculous statement that somehow, you've become a ... a what? A nymphomaniac or something? I don't believe it.'

'I don't care what you believe.'

Walker thought he'd try a different tack and he attempted a disarming smile. 'Now, if you *are* a nympho then I for one will not be complaining –'

'That's enough,' she said stiffly. 'If you say any more then I will formally request a change of terms. We obviously can't work together.'

'I'm sorry ... I didn't mean ...' He raised his hands. 'Can't we just go out and talk about it? Maybe a drink tonight?'

'No. Definitely not.' She stepped out of the office area but turned back before she left. 'Besides, I have other plans tonight.'

After she'd left, he continued to stare after her, shocked. Finally, he let out a pent-up breath. 'Other plans, is it? Let's just see who these other plans involve, shall we?'

CHAPTER FIFTEEN

ANGELA'S HONDA PULLED out of the carpark and Walker waited until the right-side blinker had moved out of view before he followed. She drove steadily through light traffic, heading east, and easy to follow. Walker made sure he left two or three cars between them. Angela made her way along Victoria Road towards the city, confirming Walker's suspicions. She had no relatives in Sydney and relatively few friends, as far as he knew. She had to be meeting someone!

She crossed the Glebe Point Bridge onto the Western Distributor and kept driving towards the CBD. She drove across George Street and he continued to follow her along William, then moved into the left lane as she approached the huge illuminated Coca-Cola billboard. 'Where are you going, Angela?' he murmured, moving his BMW down a gear as he turned into Darlinghurst Road. 'Why Kings Cross?'

Initially, he lost sight of her but then got a glimpse of her car down the first street on the left and he jerked the wheel to follow.

'Uh oh, you're going to park,' he muttered, as her tail-lights flared red. He ducked his head as he scooted past and found a spot further down, but botched the reverse park. He became aware that the clumsiness of his left hand had disappeared, so he couldn't blame that. He was annoyed with himself but also relieved that it had resolved. Right now, he didn't want to think of what caused it. By the time he reached her car she was gone, so he trotted up the street towards the bright lights at the end.

Darlinghurst Road was the usual sea of flashing lights, dingy nightclubs, crowds of wandering young men, prostitutes, pimps and porno theatres. He scanned both sides of the street then caught sight of her through a crowd about twenty metres away, walking confidently in high heels, her skirt flipping. She walked purposefully, as if she'd been here before.

He followed discreetly, wondering which bar she was going to. He also wondered what he would do when he found her with another man. Would he make a fool of himself and confront them? No, he just wanted to know.

But why Kings Cross of all places, the sex capital of the city? So much for her sex addiction! This would be the last place she'd come to if that was true.

He stopped abruptly when a terrifying thought entered his mind. Maybe she was *not* in control. Maybe she really was a sex addict! Maybe she was looking for a porn movie. Or even a prostitute? Did they have male prostitutes? Or some sort of sex club. He'd read stories about swingers, couples who swapped partners or even invited a third person to join them. Maybe she'd become a stripper? Or a prostitute herself!

She couldn't! Could she? Despite himself, he felt a rising energy and he realised he was perversely curious, although he knew he'd think differently if she really did anything like that.

Up ahead, she slowed down and a group of young men on a bucks night moved into a dingy doorway, leaving no one between her and him. She only had to look around and she'd see him. Quickly, he jumped into the doorway, following the bucks, vaguely registering the pictures of naked women displayed on the shopfront.

'Want to come see?' rasped a heavily-accented voice nearby, and Walker turned to see a young punter sporting long sideburns and wide lapels. Walker examined the premises more closely and realised it was either a strip club or an adult movie cinema. He glanced around the edge of the vestibule to see that Angela hadn't moved. She was riffling through her purse and Walker suspected she was procrastinating.

'How much?' he hesitated.

The man extended his hand and flicked his head back. 'Twenty.'

Angela had still not moved. 'What's on?' he said distractedly.

'Does it matter?' said the fellow.

Walker kept talking, keeping one eye on Angela. 'Well, for twenty bucks I'd expect something reasonably entertaining …' She'd entered the doorway and Walker scuttled up the street to investigate. Glancing back, he saw the doorman had turned his attention to the next potential customers, a nervous young couple who looked like they were out on a date.

The door that Angela had entered was set back from the road and painted jet black along with the surrounding walls, with no signs to indicate where it would lead, the surface smooth except for a black door handle. He reached out to grab it but stopped himself. What if this was a sex club? What if she *was* a prostitute? He had no right to intervene. And he'd never live down the embarrassment of finding her in such a place. He would destroy any chance of a relationship between them.

But would he want it?

He walked back to the doorman. 'Do you know what sort of place that is?'

The fellow averted his face and put on a pained expression, as if Walker had asked him his bank account details. 'Don't worry about that place. This much better. Very beautiful girls. Twenty bucks only.'

'Yes, but do you know whether it's a club of some sort? A nightclub maybe?' He hesitated. 'Or a sex club?'

The doorman flicked his head and sniffed. 'Maybe a club. Not a nightclub.' He turned away as another group of young men approached, leaving Walker alone on the street.

He walked past the door again then crossed the road and tried to see what was on the second floor, but there were no signs and all the windows were blacked out. He couldn't hear any music although there was so much noise around, there could've been a trumpet band up there and he wouldn't have heard it. He waited across the road for a few more minutes but then he attracted the attention of two skinny prostitutes who he turned down politely.

He pointed across the street. 'Do you know what that building is?'

The young women looked up then shook their heads. 'Strip joint maybe?' said one, young and pretty, with long curly hair.

A beefy man with tattoos sauntered towards them who Walker figured was their pimp, so he thanked the women again and crossed the road.

'If you change your mind,' said the other prostitute, a busty girl in a tight short dress, 'you know where to find us.'

When he reached the door, he took another look up and down the street and, seeing no one was taking notice of him, made up his mind. He turned the handle.

A set of dimly lit stairs led upwards. The carpet underfoot felt moist, as if the roof was leaking or someone had spilled something. At the top was another door, with no signs to indicate what lay beyond. He tried the latch. It was unlocked and he quietly pushed the door open.

Inside was a small dark room with chairs around the wall. On a table in the centre was a jumbled stack of old magazines. The place reminded him of a doctor's waiting room, except there was no receptionist. On the opposite wall was another door. He moved quietly to it and placed his ear against it. Nothing.

This time the door creaked as he pushed it open and he froze halfway through the action, listening intently. Mostly it was silent, although he thought he could hear running water.

He moved along a narrow corridor, which was lined with flimsy walls of the type used in cheap office buildings. Through an open door were a desk and a few chairs, again reminding him of a doctor's surgery, although a very downmarket one. And if this was a doctor's clinic, it was missing an examination couch.

He reached the end of the narrow corridor and stopped. He could definitely hear water running. A shower maybe? His impression was confirmed when he saw up the passage a door partially open with steam billowing out. Someone *was* having a shower.

Walker's mind raced. He seemed to remember reading a documentary about how prostitutes got their customers to have a shower beforehand, so they could make sure they were clean and check them for STDs. What if Angela had become a prostitute and this was one of her customers? He considered leaving. But no, he couldn't believe she would do that.

Carefully, he edged into the bathroom and peered through the steam. He could detect more than one person through the mist and he jerked back into the corridor. What if they found him? What if Angela wasn't even here? He could be arrested. But he'd come this far, he had to find out what was going on.

He crept forward into the room. On the opposite side was an open shower. In it was Angela, completely naked with her back to him.

But closer to him and out of the shower, were two people watching her. They were obviously focused on Angela and hadn't heard Walker enter. They both looked quite old. The first was a man, balding and dressed in a baggy pair of trousers and a business shirt. The other was an older woman dressed in a thick skirt and voluminous cardigan, with an untidy shock of grey hair. They both had their arms folded over their chests. As he watched, the woman scratched her head distractedly. If anything, the couple seemed bored.

'What's going on here?' he boomed. All three spun towards him.

The old woman was the first to recover. 'What are you doing in here?' she demanded. 'This is a private area.' She snapped at the man. 'Roger, how many times have I told you to lock the door when we're in session. This is the second time we've had a pervert come in off the street.'

Angela looked shocked. 'Christopher!' she gasped, as she covered herself with her arms. 'Get out. You have no right.'

The older man moved towards Walker to shepherd him away from the bathroom. 'Come on now. Out you go. This is a private session.'

'Private session,' he exclaimed. 'Calling *me* a pervert! What about you two? Watching a naked young woman in a shower. You're the perverts!'

By now Angela had wrapped a towel around her body. 'Christopher, I can't believe this,' she roared. 'How did you get here? Did you follow me?'

'What's going on here?' he demanded. 'Are these people paying you to do that?' He put his hands together, pleading. 'Angela, you don't have to do this. We could've worked through things together. We could've got professional help.'

'What are you talking about, you fool,' she shrieked. 'These two *are* helping me. *These* are the professionals.'

Walker looked dumbly from the man to the woman. 'What?'

He allowed the couple to guide him out into the hallway. Before he knew it, he was seated in the clinic cubicle on one of the chairs. The woman had thick, dark-rimmed glasses and a pen on a cord around her neck and she examined Walker calmly.

'I can see there has been a misunderstanding.' She pointed to herself then to the man. 'I'm Denise and this is my husband, Roger. We are sex therapists.'

'Sex therapists?'

'Are you a friend of Angela's?' asked the man, who also wore dark-rimmed glasses, along with a stern expression. 'You shouldn't have come barging in like that. You could've set the patient back considerably.'

'Sex therapists!' repeated Walker. He was incredulous. 'Do you ... do you have sex with her?'

'No, you idiot,' said Angela, coming through the door. She'd slipped her clothes back on but was not wearing shoes and her hair was dripping. She looked furious. 'They are helping me with my problem.'

'What problem?' he asked.

Denise addressed Angela. 'Dear, I think we should end the session tonight. Now, would you like to introduce us to your friend, since he's obviously not going to have the decency to do it himself?'

Angela seemed to calm somewhat but she refused to look at Walker and waved a hand in his direction. 'This is Christopher Walker. I work with him.' She bit her bottom lip before continuing. 'I suppose you can call him a friend.' She addressed Denise, still failing to look at Walker. 'We have been intimate. He helped me through my father's murder.'

'Oh,' Denise said with exaggerated interest and turned her attention to him. '*That* Christopher Walker. Aren't you also her boss?'

'I wouldn't call it that,' said Walker uncomfortably. 'I'm more a senior colleague. And I'm only three years older. But Angela, you still haven't told me why you're here.'

She let out an exasperated breath. 'I've discussed it with you already. It's the same as my mother.'

'Nymphomania?' he said uncertainly, looking from the man to the woman.

'We like to call it hypersexuality,' said Denise. 'Although I seriously doubt that Angela has a problem at all.' She smiled at her. 'As I've said many times, you seem to have a perfectly normal sex drive for a young woman.'

'So if she's normal,' interjected Walker, 'what was all that in the shower?'

'Just an exercise in relaxation. We were teaching Angela that it is okay to experience her body. It was one of our last sessions,' she glanced at Angela, 'although with the way it ended, now I'm not so sure.'

'I've never heard of that sort of treatment,' Walker said defensively.

Roger shifted uneasily. 'It's a cutting-edge technique. We only carry it out with the full consent of the patient and both of us are present at each session.'

'We are undertaking a clinical study to see how effective it is. Angela kindly consented. As I've said, I don't think there's a sexual issue here, at all. But we think Angela would benefit from further counselling. We're going to refer her to a counsellor closer to her home.'

Walker raised his hands to Angela. 'I just think this is all so …'

She pulled her jacket tight around her body. 'So *what?*' she demanded.

'Ridiculous,' he said.

Angela's face reddened. 'Get out!' she shouted. 'Get away from me. I don't want to ever see you again.'

'But –'

'That will be all, young man,' said Roger, standing.

Before he knew it, Walker was bundled down the stairs and out onto the street. The door slammed behind him. The spruiker from the strip joint next door waved his arm at Walker, as if he'd finally come to his senses and decided to see his show.

Ignoring him, Walker stared aghast at the black door from where he'd just been ejected.

'What the bloody hell have I done?'

CHAPTER SIXTEEN

Westmead Coroner's Inquest into the death of Dr Marcia
Links - day 2

Inquest resumed 9.00 am 2nd April 1991
Deputy State Coroner Maxwell Sleed presiding.

CORONER SLEED: Now I want to caution the members
of the press, the photographers and reporters and members
of any other news agency, regardless of what it may be, that
the same rules as set down yesterday will remain. I want to
caution the audience to be as respectful as they were
yesterday.

DR CHRISTOPHER WALKER having been previously
sworn, was further examined and testified as follows:

<u>EXAMINATION - DR CHRISTOPHER WALKER</u>

By Coroner Sleed.

Q   Doctor, you said yesterday that, just before you
        reached Doctor Links' office, you saw Doctor
        Holland Xavier walking into his office.

A   Yes.

Q   Is that right?

A   Yes.

Q   You said that he was walking away from you and
        therefore away from Doctor Links' office.

A	I said I thought that was the case, although it's difficult to be sure.
Q	You aren't sure whether it was Doctor Xavier?
A	No, it was Doctor Xavier. I'm not entirely sure he was walking away.
Q	Did you see his face?
A	I think so. I'm not sure. But I know it was Doctor Xavier.
Q	But did you see him from the rear or the front?
A	The rear, I think.
Q	Is that why you think he was walking away?
A	I guess so.
Q	Guess so?
A	Yes, I think that's the reason. I assumed he was walking away.
Q	Doctor, did Doctor Xavier come towards you and greet you perhaps?
A	No. I don't think he even saw me.
Q	So, where did he go?
A	Into his office.
Q	And where is his office in relation to Doctor Links' office?
A	It's further along the corridor. Yes, he went into his office so he must have been walking away.
Q	Are you sure about that?
A	Quite certain.
Q	Do you think he could have been coming from Doctor Links' office?
A	That I can't be sure of. He was walking away from the vicinity of her office but he might have walked past her office on the way to his office. He was almost in his office when I entered the corridor.
Q	Where were you coming from when you entered the corridor?
A	The hospital carpark. I had just parked my car.
Q	At 10.30 am? You arrived at work at 10.30?
A	On that day.

Q   Is that your normal starting time?

A   No.

Q   Did you go somewhere else after parking your car and before you reached the corridor?

A   No. Just the carpark.

Q   Was Doctor Xavier carrying anything?

A   I couldn't see.

Q   Did he have something in his hands?

A   I couldn't see.

Q   Over his shoulder perhaps?

A   I don't know.

Q   Could you see his hands?

A   I can't remember. I don't think so.

Q   So, he had his hands in front of his body. He could have been carrying something which you couldn't see.

A   I don't know. I really can't comment.

Q   How long have you known Doctor Xavier?

A   About three years.

Q   What is your relationship?

A   In what sense?

Q   Is it purely a professional relationship? Are you friends?

A   I wouldn't say we're friends. We haven't been to each other's house or anything. I would call it a professional relationship.

Q   Do you like Doctor Xavier?

A   What do you mean?

Q   Do you like him?

A   I respect him. I think he's a good oncologist. We have a good working relationship. I've always found him to be a pleasant fellow.

Q   What about Doctor Links? Did you like her?

A   I had a good working relationship with her.

Q   Is that all? Would you describe her as a pleasant work colleague?

A   Perhaps not.

Q   No?

A   I found her difficult to work with sometimes.

Q   Go on.

A   I found her to be too black and white regarding palliative care. She would often blame the oncologists for over-treating patients.

Q   As if she didn't trust your professional judgment as an oncologist?

A   I guess you could say that.

Q   So that might have caused some resentment.

A   Sometimes. But I coped with it. It was just her way.

Q   So Doctor Xavier might also have resented her.

A   You would have to ask him that.

Q   Were you present during a consultation with one of Doctor Xavier's patients – Mr Peter Shore – where there was a disagreement between Doctor Xavier and Doctor Links? This was the day before Doctor Links' death.

A   Yes, I was.

Q   What was the disagreement about?

A   About the management of the patient. Doctor Xavier was planning further chemotherapy at the patient's request. Doctor Links objected.

Q   Would you call it a heated discussion?

A   Yes.

Q   Tempers did rise? Including yours? What was your role?

A   Doctor Xavier asked me to be there to offer support. But my temper was fine. I disagreed with Doctor Links but I wouldn't say I was angry.

Q   What about Doctor Xavier? Was he angry?

A   I wouldn't say angry. But you would have to ask him.

Q   What about the patient? Was he angry?

A   No, I found him very logical and calm.

Q   And the patient's son? Jason Shore. Was he angry?

A   Patient's relatives often get upset in this sort of situation.

Q   Was he angry with Doctor Links? Were angry words exchanged?

A   I think Jason Shore was more shocked with Doctor Links' attitude than angry.

Q   So he wasn't angry.

A   I don't think so.

Q   You told the police that Doctor Links always wore a gold necklace with a fish pendant, is that correct?

A   She was always wearing it when I saw her. It was a gift from a famous colleague.

Q   A gift. So she would never take it off?

A   I don't know about that. But I always saw her with it.

Q   You said yesterday that when you were walking past Doctor Links' office, you sensed there was a fire behind the door.

A   That's correct.

Q   How did you know that?

A   The door was very hot. The handle.

Q   What made you feel the handle? Were you intending to enter?

A   No, the air temperature was raised. I knew there was something wrong.

Q   So you felt the handle was hot and realised there was a fire.

A   I didn't know for sure. I tried to open it but it was locked.

Q   Are you sure it was locked?

A   I thought it was. I told the police that as well. But in retrospect it could have been the timbers swollen from the heat that made the door stick.

Q   Perhaps it was not locked.

A   But Detective Darling later confirmed that it was locked from the inside.

Q   This was after you had kicked the door in.

A   That's correct.

Q   How did you open the door? Did you have help?

A   I called but there was no one there. As I said yesterday, I kicked at it then ran at it with my shoulder and eventually the timber cracked and it opened.

Q   Did you look and check whether the lock was activated?

A   No.

Q   Did you get any idea whether the lock had been engaged.

A   No, the room was full of fire.

Q   The whole room?

A   Well no, just the chair and parts of the desk.

Q   And Doctor Links?

A   Like I said yesterday, she was gone. Or rather, most of her. You saw the photos. Her leg remained, and her hand on the desk. And a skull.

Q   How did you know it was hers?

A   The leg still had her shoe, which I knew to be hers.

Q   And the hand?

A   It had a cigarette between the fingers.

Q   Was the cigarette alight?

A   Yes, I'm fairly sure it was. Although it could have been burnt by the fire.

Q   And you mentioned an odour.

A   Yes. There was the burnt flesh smell – like burnt meat. But there was another smell – something flammable. I thought it was alcohol.

Q   Alcohol?

A   It reminded me of Drambuie.

Q   The liqueur.

A   Yes.

Q   Could it have been something else? Petrol?

A   It didn't smell like petrol.

Q   You told the police that you thought you smelt alcohol on Doctor Links' breath while working with her.

A		I thought I did. But it didn't smell like that. Now I'm not sure.
Q		Could it have smelled like model airplane fuel?
A		I don't know. I've never smelt airplane fuel.
CORONER SLEED: That is all. We will have a break and reconvene at 1 PM. Thank you.

Inquest resumed 1.00 pm 2nd April 1991

EXAMINATION - SENIOR SERGEANT DETECTIVE BARRY DARLING

By Coroner Sleed.
Q		Senior Sergeant Detective Darling, you have heard the testimony of Dr Christopher Walker, and the record of your interview with him regarding the death has been provided. I would like to ask about your findings of the examination of Doctor Links' office when you first arrived at the scene.
A		What aspect of the findings?
Q		Did you smell an odour?
A		There was the smell of burnt timber and plastic and burnt flesh.
Q		Anything else? Anything other than you would expect to find when a body was incinerated?
A		I've never smelt an incinerated body before.
Q		Was there anything that smelt like alcohol as described by Doctor Walker? He mentioned Drambuie.
A		I can't say that I did.
Q		Can't say?
A		No, I did not.
Q		Nothing like a flammable liquid – petrol or some other liquid?
A		No.
Q		Model airplane fuel?

A   No. But it was at least thirty minutes after the fire had been extinguished. The fumes could have dissipated.

Q   You were present yesterday when both Constable David Jones and Doctor Jocelyn Banks also testified that they did not smell anything like that.

A   Yes, I heard their examination.

Q   Was there any evidence of fuel found in the remains on forensic examination?

A   You would have to ask Doctor Banks that but I was told not.

Q   You have submitted a statement regarding your questioning of the deceased's son, Jason Shore.

A   That is correct.

Q   In it you state that Jason Shore is an active member of the Macquarie Model Airplane Club. You visited the club approximately two weeks ago and there you confirmed that the pilots – if that's what they're called – use glow fuel, which is a mixture of highly flammable chemicals.

A   That's correct.

Q   You checked on Jason Shore's whereabouts at the time of Doctor Links' death. According to the nurses' testimony, he had left his father's bed for no more than ten minutes around that time, although there was some uncertainty regarding the time of day and the period. The staff at the coffee shop, which he frequented, could not be definitive as to whether he had attended on the morning of the death.

A   That is correct.

Q   We will examine Jason Shore tomorrow. Tell me about the lock. You wrote in the report that you thought the lock had been engaged. We saw photos of the door and lock yesterday. Can you please explain how these locks work?

A   It's called a multipoint lock. The door handle is separate to the lock. The lock itself is a thumb turn cylinder. Unlocked, the door can be opened and closed without a key. If the door is locked you need a key externally, but the lock can be turned internally with a thumb turn. You can lock the door from the inside using the thumb turn.

Q So if there was a fire, for example, the occupant could egress without using a key. And I understand the only way to lock the door externally is with a key. You can't lock the door as you are leaving and pull it shut?

A That's correct. It's to reduce the chance of the occupant locking the door and leaving the key inside.

Q So if someone other than Doctor Links was in the office, lit a fire, then left, they could only lock the door with a key.

A That is correct.

Q We have an affidavit from hospital security that states that only two keys for that door exist. One key was held in security and has not been released. The other was issued to Doctor Links. Was that key found?

A Yes. It was on the ground near the remains of the body. We assume she was holding it and it dropped to the floor during the fire.

Q Or she may have had it in a pocket or on her clothing somewhere.

A I suppose so.

Q Are there any windows in the office?

A Just one, which is fixed shut and cannot be opened without special tools. It's closed for the air conditioning.

Q Was there any other way out of the room? Through the ceiling?

A There are panels that allow access to a tight ceiling space where pipes run. It's too tight for anyone other than a small child to access.

Q   Was there any evidence that these panels had been moved?

A   No. We examined them thoroughly.

Q   So there is no way a person could have been in the office with Doctor Links, lit a fire, then exited and locked the door.

A   Not that I could determine.

Q   How do you know the door was locked?

A   The dead bolt was extruding.

Q   The dead bolt is the part of the lock that engages with the door frame to lock the door.

A   That is correct.

Q   And this was extruded, as it would be, if the door was locked.

A   Yes.

Q   How do you know it wasn't locked after the door was forced? These locks can be locked from the inside. Anyone could have done so after the event.

A   No, they couldn't. The fire had damaged the lock so it was stuck open. That is, in the locked position. The metal had heated to a degree that some of the internal components may have fused. I'm not sure of the details of how that might happen. But both Constable Jones and I tried separately and on multiple occasions to turn the lock, both with the thumb turn and the key. We could not budge it.

Q   So the door must have been locked before or during the fire.

A   That is my belief.

Q   Did you find a gold necklace in the room?

A   No.

Q   You searched thoroughly?

A   Yes, and not just Constable Jones and me. The entire forensic team did. Everything was bagged. There was no necklace.

Q   Could it have melted?

A   There would be evidence. The key didn't melt,
        although that was made of harder metal than gold.
        But there should at least have been a molten blob of
        gold.
Q   So, in your opinion, was she wearing it at the time of
        the fire?
A   No.

Inquest resumed 3.00 pm 2nd April 1991

EXAMINATION - DOCTOR JOCELYN BANKS

By Coroner Sleed.
Q   Doctor Banks, we have gone over your impressive
        credentials yesterday so we will not repeat them. You
        told us yesterday that you performed a forensic
        examination of the contents of the office of Doctor
        Links, both in situ, on the day of the fire, and later by
        autopsy. You have confirmed that the remains found
        were that of Doctor Marcia Links and that the cause
        of death was incineration.
A   Yes, that is correct.
Q   From your examination of the remains and any other
        items from the office, did you find any evidence of
        flammable chemicals?
A   Multiple samples of the remains – the leg, the hand –
        and other items such as the shoe, the carpet, the
        chair, the desk and others, were sent to DAL for
        forensic examination.
Q   That's the Division of Analytical Laboratories at
        Lidcombe.
A   Yes. They found no evidence of flammable
        chemicals.
Q   Glow fuel?

A   Glow fuel is a mixture of nitromethane, methanol, and castor oil. None of those chemicals were found except traces of castor oil.

Q   Yes?

A   Castor oil is often prescribed by palliative care physicians as a laxative. It's also used in certain foods. Finding a trace of castor oil in this setting would not be unusual.

Q   But none of the other chemicals?

A   None at all.

Q   Is it possible for them to have burned away completely?

A   I'm not an expert in that area but I'm told that it would be unlikely.

Q   Unlikely?

A   Yes.

Q   We will have the scientist from DAL and a forensic pathologist who specialises in pyrotechnics testify tomorrow. But in your opinion, what was the cause of the fire?

A   Spontaneous combustion.

Q   Can you explain what that is?

A   Spontaneous human combustion is a term that refers to the burning of a human body without any apparent external source of ignition.

Q   Is this an accepted forensic diagnosis?

A   It is contentious. Some claim that it does not exist, although there have been numerous thoroughly documented cases that have a common theme. Victims are usually elderly, overweight Caucasian women who are socially isolated and have consumed a large amount of alcohol. Strangely, while parts of the body, usually the torso, have been reduced to ashes, other areas such as the distal limbs and head are preserved. This also applies to adjacent clothing and objects such as furniture. It is the latter that has led to scepticism as to how sufficient heat could be generated to reduce parts of a body to ash and yet leave adjacent tissues and materials untouched. Dark and greasy soot coating the walls are a typical finding.

Q   Were these features present here?

A   Yes, all of them.

Q   Were there any other findings?

A   We checked for soot in the trachea and low blood carboxyhemoglobin levels, which might have suggested that the deceased had already been murdered or had died from some other cause and then the body incinerated post mortem. None of these were present.

Q   If the deceased had been doused in flammable liquid then set alight, would the features be similar to the ones you found?

A   Yes, but as I said, there was no evidence of flammable chemicals.

Q   Is there a known cause for spontaneous combustion?

A   No one really knows how it occurs. The favoured hypothesis is the so called 'wick' or 'candle effect' where a body smoulders at relatively low temperatures with fat soaking through splitting skin into the adjacent fabric. It has been shown that a cloth wick in melted human fat can continue to burn at temperatures as low as 24 degrees centigrade, which is proposed as an explanation for the limitation of the size of the fire and the preservation of adjacent body parts and clothing. The possibility of alcohol spilling onto clothes and acting as an accelerant may be another possibility, particularly in smokers.

CORONER SLEED: That is all. This inquest will reconvene at 9 AM tomorrow. Thank you.

CHAPTER SEVENTEEN

THE MOON WAS full and bright but the streets of The Rocks were dark and heavy with late summer heat. Inside his terrace on Lower Fort Street, Walker sat hunched over a laminated kitchen table, a half-finished stubby clasped in hands slick with sweat. A lazy blowfly buzzed from wall to wall, seeking escape from the stifling air of the small room while Archie, the shaggy Siberian cat, sat regally near the back door, front legs together, bushy tail flicking, staring at Walker with his usual emotionless face, as if he was a headmaster examining a wayward student.

The radio was on and popular music played in the background. Walker was a fan of Triple J and this was the evening of the week when Richard Kingsmill played new releases. The smooth-voiced presenter sounded more excited than usual and promised to play a new record in its entirety, just released the week before in the UK. Walker was about to switch it off when the record started – soft, haunting electronic music that gradually became louder, followed by a cultured female voice who called herself Enigma, telling him to turn off the light and relax for the next hour. Walker's finger hovered over the switch, waiting to see what came next. Gregorian monks chanting was something he didn't expect. He sat back on his chair. The room was already dark. He then spent the next forty minutes in a near trance listening to the spiritual electronic music, as if it were a revelation. Finally, the wafting pipes faded away, leaving him exhausted and sorry for himself.

Finally, he stirred. 'Archie, I can't continue like this. I can't sleep, I'm useless at work and I'm getting nowhere with Angela. She'll never see me again after what I did. And to make things even crazier, Wendy tried to apologise to me!'

He lifted a leaden hand towards the cat. 'What for? For all I know, everything Wendy said about Flea is true. Maybe I let her die.' His throat worked silently for a moment before he continued, his voice hoarse. 'Maybe I *did* eat her flesh.' He paused as if waiting for a response, then shook his head. 'I just can't remember.'

Archie abruptly became interested in the crack where the kitchen bench met the tiled floor – a cockroach, no doubt. Walker gave a sigh full of weariness and cradled his head in his hands, elbows on the table, the beer forgotten. 'All I know is, until I find out the truth about her, I can't continue. I must find out, for good or bad. If somehow I let her die …' He swallowed. 'Or if I ate part of her to survive … then at least I would know. Maybe I wouldn't be able to live with the truth.' He stared down at his fists, which were now clenched on the tabletop. 'But what I have now is not a life.' He raised his eyes to the Siberian. 'This is hell. Better to be dead if things don't change!'

The cat licked itself.

Walker lurched to his feet. 'I'm going to the pub.'

At first, he headed towards the Hero of Waterloo but kept walking past when he saw James standing at the bar. He'd been rude to him the other night and he didn't feel like apologising. Down the road was the Lord Nelson but that brought back memories of Peter Runsack. Besides, it was a tourist pub. He wanted a real one. When he reached the Lord Nelson, he crossed the road and walked a bit further to the Captain Cook. The pub was no-frills and full of locals who came to drink and talk and do business. It was also a pub where you could sit in a corner and be ignored.

He ordered a Tooheys from the tap then looked around and spied a perfect table at the back in the dark and made his way to it. But a moment after he'd flopped into the plastic chair, he sensed a figure towering over him. He raised his eyes slowly – stained suit trousers, crumpled jacket, shirt stretched over a fat belly.

'Kit,' said Bruce Rowntree, his voice a cross between a wheeze and a cough. Rowntree was balding with a sunburnt face and had the nose of a drinker. As usual, he had a fag hanging out of the corner of his mouth. 'Nice to see you gracing us with your presence. What's the occasion?' He glanced around. 'Meeting your girlfriend?'

Walker was initially startled, thinking Cassandra – or worse, Angela – had come through the door and he jerked around, keeping his head low. Then he realised it was one of Rowntree's sick jokes.

'Wendy's not coming if that's what you mean.'

'Good.' He pulled out a chair opposite. 'I'll join you then. Can't have you drinking alone.'

'Bruce, if you don't mind –'

'Now, now.' He waved his hands dismissively. 'I've been in this job long enough to know a troubled soul.' He pointed his cigarette at Walker's chest. 'And you're one, sunshine, believe me. You look like you need someone to talk to.'

'What job is that?' asked Walker sarcastically, trying to change the subject.

'Unions.' Rowntree lounged back in his chair and dragged on the stub of the cigarette. 'It's not all meetings and going on strike, you know. There's the pastoral aspects of the job, as well.' He blew smoke out through his nose. 'I'm told I'm pretty good at it.'

'Pastoral? You mean like a priest?'

'*Exactly* like a priest. But without all the churchy mumbo jumbo. A lot of people need the care but not the Christ, I like to say.' His dry lips stretched into a grin at his own joke.

Despite himself, Walker laughed. He took a long sip of his beer while he appraised the union bagman. What did he have to lose? 'All right, Bruce, I'll tell you my problems.'

Rowntree raised his arms expansively. 'I'm all ears.'

Walker began talking and didn't stop for over an hour. He'd no intention of telling Rowntree everything – about the possible flesh-eating, for one, nor about how he thought his brain had been infected by a slow virus. But he told him more than he thought he would. And to Rowntree's credit, he listened carefully without interrupting, except for occasional well-placed questions of clarification. Walker spoke about Flea drowning and how now there were suspicious circumstances. He described his time of delirium in the New Guinea jungle and about how Bruce Darling had gone back. How his old friend seemed to blame him for Felicity's death. He talked about Angela – how he liked her but how they never seemed to connect. About Cassandra – how he thought she had genuine feelings for him but how he couldn't bring himself to reciprocate.

Finally, he stopped talking. He felt exhausted, but also some of the dread he'd carried had lightened. Rowntree had sat listening, puffing on cigarette after cigarette, and now Walker could see his packet of Marlboros was just about empty. He looked at Rowntree, not knowing what he would say.

'Well, I think there's only one answer,' he said, after he'd sat thoughtfully for some minutes, puffing on his last cigarette.

'What's that?' Walker gave a humourless laugh. 'Top myself?'

He shook his head as if he took the suggestion seriously. 'No, no. That's not the answer, Kit.' He looked Walker squarely in the eyes. 'I think you need to go back.'

'Back? Back where?'

'To New Guinea.'

Walker flopped back in his chair. 'Are you serious? What for?'

'That's where the problem started. That's where it will have to end. No sense sitting here a thousand miles away thinking everything will sort itself out. There are mysteries there that can only be unravelled by going back to the source.'

Walker stared into the distance. 'Back to New Guinea. Back to where Flea died.' He looked at Rowntree. 'You know what, Bruce, maybe you're right. Maybe I have to go back and speak to the people. The villagers will still be there. They might have seen something. And they won't tell anyone unless you ask them directly. I know them.'

Rowntree nodded. 'See, you're already thinking.' He tapped him on the shoulder. 'And look at you. You've got a bit of your old energy back.'

Walker shook his head. He didn't believe what he was thinking of doing. 'Back to New Guinea, eh? I'll have to go alone, of course.'

'I'll come with you, if you want.' Rowntree coughed out a lungful of cigarette smoke. 'Need a bit of a holiday.' His beady eyes flitted around the pub. 'And it would be opportune to disappear for a little while, if you know what I mean. Lay low, as they say.'

Walker knew he wasn't serious. 'You'd never make it, Bruce. They've banned smoking on flights a few years ago.'

He looked surprised. 'They never! Why would they do a stupid thing like that?'

'Might ban it in pubs one day, you never know.'

'Bullshit!' Rowntree stabbed a nicotine-stained finger at Walker's chest. 'That, I guarantee, will never happen. Not on my watch.'

'I've got an old friend there,' continued Walker, ignoring his outburst. 'I'll contact him and see if he can come with me. We worked together in the TB clinics. He was with us in the last village we visited before Flea died.'

'Good idea. Now you're thinking.'

'I'm going back to find out the truth, even if it kills me.' Walker licked his lips. 'And if it does, I'll accept it.' He looked across the table nervously at Rowntree. 'The only thing I'm worried about, Bruce, is that now you know all my secrets. I hope you don't use them against me.'

He leaned back and raised his arms again. 'Kit, I know you think that you're the Ghost Who fuckin' Walks but when it comes to the Phantom, there's no one around here that's more like him than yours truly.' He grinned and took another drag on the stub of his fag. 'If we're talking about using talents for good rather than evil, then I'm your man.' He nodded his head sideways and grimaced. 'Unless you're a union scab or a Liberal dipshit, then I'll definitely use what I've got to stuff it right up your arse, if you get me drift.' He pointed at Walker stiffly. 'And before you say anything smart, I'm not talking about me cock.'

He stood up and looked down at him. 'You know what, Bruce, you've really helped me. Thank you.' He offered his hand and Rowntree magnanimously took it.

'All in a day's work, young Kit. All in a day's work.' He stubbed his fag into the table. 'Now you can buy me a packet of Marlboros and us both a couple of beers.'

CHAPTER EIGHTEEN

THE DAY AFTER the inquest, Darling received a call at his office. He listened carefully, grunted a few times then replaced the handset on in its cradle.

'Spontaneous combustion, Jones. Who would have believed it?'

'You have to admit,' said Jones, 'the evidence against Jason Shore was pretty thin.'

'Apparently it was the lock that saved him. My testimony saying the door was locked and that no one could have locked it from the outside was very believable, according to the court registrar.'

'Argued against yourself then.'

'I guess so. Anyway, that's that. Can't do anything about it. Can't say I seriously thought Shore had done it.'

The phone rang again and he picked it up. It was Fred Bowles. He wanted to see him. Darling called back as he left, 'You hold the fort, Jones. I'm off to The Rocks.'

An hour later, Darling pulled into a police parking spot on George Street and made his way along the Nurses Walk to The Rocks Police Station.

Superintendent Fred Bowles greeted him in his office and asked him to take a seat.

'Your story checks out,' said Fred, his jowls wobbling. 'The South African is Kronig Harlow. As far as we can tell, he's ex-military. He arrived in Australia on a tourist visa two days before Runsack's death and left the day he died.'

'Where to?'

'There's the thing.' Bowles gave a queer smile, his mouth disproportionately small in his flabby face. 'You'll never guess.'

He gave a look to say he wasn't going to try.

'New Guinea,' said Bowles, his grin widening in satisfaction at the effect it had on the younger officer.

Darling didn't know what to say. While he was struggling to comprehend the significance, Bowles continued. He was still smiling as if he was Father Christmas handing out presents.

'And there's more. The two girls you mentioned – do you know which country they arrived from?'

'New Guinea?' Darling said numbly.

'Spot on!' exclaimed Bowles, slapping his hands gleefully as if he'd won the lottery.

'Do you think they're working together?'

Now Bowles became less excited. 'Don't know. But the Saffie is definitely a person of interest. Runsack's briefcase is gone. It's not in his hotel room and it's not at the bottom of the harbour. Kronig Harlow was witnessed following Peter Runsack from the hotel in the morning. And we have the story from Kit's Leb mate. It's third-hand and won't stack up in court, but it was enough to convince a magistrate to issue an arrest warrant.'

'What about the women? Are they South African?'

Bowles shook his head. 'Pretty sure they're Australians, at least the white girl. They both had Aussie accents according to the hotel staff. We think they used fake names. They showed Australian passports as ID in the hotel but we think they might be fake. They used them to enter from PNG but their names don't link up with any other records.'

'Sounds sophisticated. How are they tied up in this?'

Bowles grunted. 'The dark woman might be Aboriginal, but given Harlow going to PNG, she might be from there. The Aussie accent counts against it though.'

'Torres Strait Islander maybe?' suggested Darling.

'What are they exactly? That's halfway between Cape York and New Guinea, isn't it? Are they Australian or PNG?'

'Australian,' said Darling. 'But I think they look different to mainland Aboriginals.'

'I guess she could be from Torres Strait,' Bowles said uncertainly.

'Could they be working with Harlow?'

'Maybe. Strange thing is, they've both disappeared. No one knows where they've got to. If they left the country then they've used a different set of passports.'

'Do you have warrants for their arrest as well?'

Bowles shook his head. 'Not at this stage. But we're definitely going to keep on their tails.'

'What now?' Darling was beginning to wonder why Bowles had summoned him. 'Fred, it's nice of you to keep me in the loop but why didn't you tell me all this on the phone?'

Bowles gave a sneaky smirk. 'Thing is, we need to send someone to PNG to chase Harlow.'

'That would be a Federal Police job.'

'Yes,' said Bowles. 'And no. The crime was perpetrated in New South Wales so it's really up to us. The feds need to be involved but they're more to do with counter-terrorism and national security. They have a presence in PNG, but a murder that happened in our jurisdiction is predominantly our responsibility.'

Darling tilted his head. 'So you need to send someone?'

Bowles nodded. 'But I can't spare anyone. The spike in drug crimes at the moment is killing us.'

'So?'

'So, given your interest …'

Darling stifled the thrill rising in his chest. 'You want me to go?' He lurched upright, unable to contain his excitement. 'You'll have to clear it with my superiors.'

'Already have.' Bowles pulled a long black wallet from his drawer and threw it onto the desk. 'Your ticket to Port

Moresby. It leaves tomorrow at 10 am. I'll get one of the feds to meet you at the airport. They've been briefed already.'

Darling thrust out his hand for Fred Bowles to shake. 'Thank you very much, sir. You won't regret this.'

'Just catch the bastard, Wendy. That's all you need to do.'

CHAPTER NINETEEN

AT THREE IN the afternoon the next day, Darling touched down at Jacksons International Airport in Port Moresby and was met by a young male officer at the arrival gate. He introduced himself as Constable Peter Token, a tall, gangly fellow in his late twenties. He was wearing an Australian Federal Police uniform with a large red and blue patch on the shoulder sporting two logos – one for Australia, one for PNG. Token led him to an unmarked Toyota Landcruiser, complete with snorkel and bull-bar.

'Kronig Harlow's entry into PNG was registered by customs,' said Token as he pulled away. 'Port Moresby's a small place, so it was pretty easy to find out where he went.'

'Good,' said Darling, trying to sound as if he had everything under control. He realised he was out of his depth in PNG, with no local knowledge whatsoever, and he would have to rely on the AFP to find Harlow. But it was he who would arrange the arrest and escort him back to Australia. 'Where is he?'

'He's still in Port Moresby. We're having him followed.'

'Okay, I have an Australian warrant for his arrest and a provisional arrest request and extradition papers for the local cops.'

'Good. First things first, we need a local magistrate to issue a local arrest warrant based on those documents. That's best done through the local constabulary.' Token took a quick left and Darling saw a street sign that read Morea-Tobo Road. 'The station's not far but I thought I'd take you on the scenic route.'

On both sides of the roads stood derelict houses made of thrown-together corrugated iron and poorly painted timber planks. Youths clustered on street corners and watched them as they drove by, and Darling sensed a wall of threat and disquiet, even from the safety of the moving vehicle.

'One of the settlements,' said Token. 'Mostly highlanders who've come to the city. The *raskols* used to come from places like this but now they're all over, and not just in Port Moresby.'

'Why are there so many gangs?'

Token swayed his head and puffed out his cheeks as if the full explanation would take an eternity. 'Young men from the highlands attracted by money. *Bisnis*, they call it. But when they get here, they find they're at the bottom of the barrel. They can't get a job so they join a gang. Australia did a lot of good for PNG but it also did a lot of bad. This was our only colony and we ran it like the British ran theirs last century. Excluded the locals from the money, made them servants, segregated our women away from them. I guess it's their way of trying to gouge back some of what they feel is theirs in the first place. Tanked up on beer, they steal as much as they can, then go back to the highlands. Murder and rape are common. The *raskol* gangs have been getting worse and worse. Any expats still here live behind walls with guard dogs and alarms. Most have gone. When we left in '75, the local coppers were ill-equipped to deal with the gangs. Still are. There's not enough police and the public don't trust them.' The young constable flicked his head to Darling. 'Is that enough for you? It's obviously much more complex than that but that's the gist of it.'

'You seem to have thought a lot about it.'

'Have to. I'm doing it as part of my Masters of Philosophy.'

'Wow,' said Darling. 'Is that something you need to be a fed?'

'No, not at all. But I want to. And it helps to understand some of the issues we're dealing with.'

They had passed into a more salubrious part of the town and soon Token turned into a fenced area beside a squat grey building, with a sign identifying it as the Royal Papua New Guinea Constabulary Headquarters. Inside, Darling was introduced to a number of the local officers who took his bundle of documents and agreed to get onto it right away.

'The yacht club down the road is usually good for dinner,' said Token. 'I'll pick you up from your hotel. Whatever you do, don't walk around by yourself, especially after dark. At the least, you'll be robbed.'

'And the worst?'

'Murdered.'

'Nice place,' said Darling.

'You'll get used to it. Apart from the heat and the violence, it's a great little town. Oh, there's also the dengue fever and malaria. But apart from that, it's a nice place.'

The next day, the PNG police had not made any progress. They needed a magistrate to issue a local arrest warrant based on the Australian documentation but they'd got caught up with local issues – an expat's house broken into, a handful of rapes, a stabbing at a place called Hanubada.

'We will do it today, *kwiktaim*,' said one officer, flashing a reassuring smile. 'No worries.'

With nothing else to do, Darling hazarded a walk down to Ella Beach and on the way passed St Mary's Cathedral, a modest utilitarian building set back from the water's edge. The beach was a narrow strip of sand littered with rubbish and seaweed, and Darling lingered for a while, watching a group of young boys diving off the rocks.

He got back to the station in the late afternoon to find that still nothing had been arranged with a magistrate.

'The judge is very busy today,' said the same officer, smiling again. 'There are many cases.' He turned to a colleague and there ensued a short conversation in a language Darling did not understand. The officer turned back to Darling. 'Tomorrow. The judge will be free tomorrow.'

Darling hunted down Peter Token who threw his hands up vaguely. 'Something you'll have to get used to,' he said resignedly. 'They work to a different drum here.' He opened a file on his desk. 'We've found some information about Kronig Harlow though.'

'Oh?' said Darling, taking a seat opposite.

'South African national,' Token continued, 'first arrived in January. Is said to be advising the government on the trouble in Bougainville.' He looked up from his folder. 'The BRA – Bougainville Revolutionary Army – declared the island of Bougainville to be independent from Papua New Guinea in May last year. There are rumours the PNG government will land a force on the island in the next few months.'

'Civil war?'

'Sort of. It's all about the Panguna copper mine owned by Rio Tinto. The PNG government has a twenty percent share and the revenue from the mine is their biggest income. The Bougainvilleans don't like the mainland labourers. Call them red skins. There's been fighting for the last few years and the Royal Constabulary have been involved. PNG pulled out of the island early last year hoping it would diffuse the issue but the leader of the BRA did a backflip and declared independence. Now the PNG government has its knickers in a knot. There's no way they will forego that amount of money. The question is, how hard will they go? Confidentially, they've asked Australia for help but we won't have a bar of it. There's talk of PNG bringing in mercenaries.'

'And you think Harlow has something to do with it?'

'That's our intelligence.' He examined his folder again. 'Harlow works for a mercenary unit out of the UK called

Bosses For Freedom. Basically, they sell their guns to the highest bidder.'

'So what's he doing here in Port Moresby?'

'That we don't know for sure but we think it has something to do with Bougainville.'

'If he is working for the PNG government then Peter Runsack's murder is looking more and more complicated.'

'Exactly.'

CHAPTER TWENTY

THE NEXT DAY Walker landed at Jacksons Airport after a four-hour flight on Air Niugini from Sydney to a muggy thirty-one degrees, not much different from the weather he'd left behind. The day before, he'd given notice of extended leave from the hospital, much to the distress of the head of medical oncology.

Before he left, Walker had also phoned one of his old colleagues from the DOTS team who he'd worked with back in 1986. The Directly Observed Treatment Strategy was the primary method to control tuberculosis in PNG, and he and Felicity had been involved with training the health workers in the highlands who travelled from village to village, ensuring that those diagnosed with TB took their prescribed medication.

After a two-hour wait, he boarded a Dash 7 four-engine turbo-prop bound for Goroka and, after a ninety-minute flight, made his way to the newly renovated Bird of Paradise Hotel, a short walk from the airport. He'd packed light, taking the same sixty-litre blue Berghuas backpack that he'd used six years ago, which was more than enough for his needs. The fresh mountain air, the rag-tag buildings, the jumble of old trucks and four-wheel drives, the indolent locals standing or sitting on the roadside, and the familiar weight of the straps on his shoulders brought back memories of his time here with Felicity, feelings that flickered from fondness to disturbing in an instant.

He'd organised to meet Justin Namah, his former colleague, for dinner in the hotel that evening, which was still a few hours away. So after checking in, he wandered down to the Papindo Top Town, a large supermarket a short walk along the main street. The shelves were mostly stacked with canned food and non-perishables but there was a small meat section and, to his delight, a new coffee shop where he wasted an hour tasting the local brew. There were extensive coffee plantations to the south of Goroka and Highlands Blue was one of his favourite blends.

Justin Namah had a typical highlander appearance, with deep-set eyes, a generous nose and mouth, and an easy smile, and they hugged each other energetically when they met in the foyer of the hotel that evening. They'd spent over a year together touring the south-eastern highlands and Walker had a momentary pang of guilt for not keeping in touch with his old friend. But they were soon talking as if they'd only parted company a few days before, regaling each other with memories of their time together but each careful to avoid any mention of the third member of their old team.

But like a satellite caught in the tug of Earth's atmosphere, the topics eventually spiralled down to the reason that had brought Walker back. Justin had finished speaking about a patient they'd treated in the last village the trio had visited — a child with TB involving lymph nodes in the neck. On a previous visit, after spending considerable time convincing the parents the child was not sick due to sorcery, they'd sent a sample of the lymph node to the Queensland Mycobacterium Reference Laboratory in Brisbane. When the result had come back positive for mycobacterium tuberculosis, they'd commenced the child on a short course of antibiotics as part of a clinical trial that was being run out of the Port Moresby paediatric department. On their last visit to the small village of Urai, south of Purosa, they'd been encouraged by the child's improvement, with all signs of lymph node enlargement having resolved.

It was in that village six years ago where they had met Alf Runsack, the Australian geologist who was finishing off his survey of the region. They spoke about him briefly but Justin did not mention anything about Alf's purported murder, so

Walker kept the recent events of the brother, Peter Runsack, to himself. After Urai they had parted company, Justin travelling back to Purosa, and Walker and Felicity going north-west to Misapi Mission.

There followed a long pause as both men gazed out from the open veranda at the vista of the mountains to the south. Finally, Justin turned back, his face sombre.

'I was sorry to hear about Felicity.'

Walker failed to meet his friend's eye, keeping his attention on the southern range. 'That's why I've come back. I want to find out what happened to her.'

'What do you mean?' Justin looked surprised. 'She drowned. Along with your guide. We all know it.'

'That's what I thought too. But a friend of mine … well, an old friend who is now a cop, has different ideas. He went to the hut where I was … after I nearly drowned. I don't remember much about it. But he found stuff, evidence that he thinks tells a different story.'

'What story?'

Walker stared at the mountains, to the place where everything had happened, so long ago. 'I want to go back there. See for myself. Maybe it will trigger memories.' He looked at Justin. 'I have to know.'

'Know what?'

'Know whether I did something that led to her death.' He hesitated. 'And other things.' Walker held his friend's eyes in his. 'Will you help me?'

Justin didn't hesitate. 'Of course, I will. We'll go together. Do you know where it is?'

'I can work it out. I have maps.'

'When shall we leave?'

'As soon as we can. Tomorrow?'

Justin thought for a moment, then smiled brightly. 'Sure, I can do it. Not tomorrow. Give me a few days. I need to do a few things. We can leave early on Monday morning.'

CHAPTER TWENTY-ONE

THAT DAY, DARLING was told a familiar story by the same officer he'd been dealing with – the local team had not had a chance to present the documents to a magistrate. There had been a storming of an expat compound by *raskols* overnight, a few murders and another half-dozen rapes reported.

'Is that normal?' asked Darling. 'That many rapes?'

The officer shook his head, as if he too were surprised. 'It is true. Too many rapes are being reported. And wife bashings as well. Before, they would not be reported. The *wantok* would sort it themselves. Now, they expect the police to solve all their problems.' The fellow made an exasperated gesture, as if he could not understand what the world was coming to.

Darling was momentarily rendered speechless. 'Sort it themselves? But rape is a crime. These men must be brought to justice.'

The officer looked at Darling as if he were a naive child. 'Which men? In the town, almost *all* men do it. It is common for husbands to beat their wives. The women must do as their husbands say. And the *raskols* rape women for initiation. Everyone knows it. The women are stupid for being caught alone.'

'That is the most ridiculous thing I have ever heard. Does every policeman think like you?'

'Of course,' said the officer. 'This is not Australia. We have a different way here.'

'Are you saying it is okay for women to be raped?'

The officer shook his finger. 'I did not say that. Sometimes it is wrong but it not for us to say so. It is up to their own *wantok*, their community to control them. We are not their masters.'

Darling shook his head in disbelief. It was clear there were different values at play. 'When will you take my documents to the magistrate,' he asked through gritted teeth.

'When the magistrate is not busy,' came the firm reply, the helpful smile gone.

'And when do you expect that will be?'

'Hard to say,' he said. 'Could be a long time.' He shrugged. 'It's the way we do it. *Mekim bisnis pasin.*' His smile widened further when he saw Darling's growing rage. 'Maybe you should go home and leave it to us.'

Darling found Peter Token at his desk on the next floor. 'These clowns are being obstructive, not lazy,' he snapped.

Token looked at Darling, his young face troubled. 'Yes, I think there's something deeper here than we first suspected.'

'What do you mean?'

'My boss is telling me that we are getting pressure from higher up to drop it.'

'Higher up? In the police?'

'Higher. From up the road.' Token jerked his thumb through the window, which framed a treed park with a large building beyond. 'Government House.'

Darling peered silently at the building, which was partially obscured by the trees. 'From the prime minister?' he finally asked.

'Not the prime minister but it is hard to say who. Certainly a government official or a senior public servant.'

'If the PNG government is involved then this is obviously bigger than the simple murder of an Australian. I've got a feeling that we're going to get nowhere with our current approach.'

'I've come to the same conclusion,' said Token grimly.

Darling wandered out of the rear door of the police station into the adjacent park. He needed to gather his thoughts and make a plan. Maybe it was not worth staying? On top of the hill sat Government House and a long driveway ran alongside the park towards it. He stood watching for some time, wondering what the government could have to do with a killer like Kronig Harlow. But as he turned to re-enter the police station, Peter Token rushed out of the door.

'Just got a call. It's Harlow. He's driving towards Government House.'

Darling looked back at the road just as a Toyota Hilux drove past towards the building.

Harlow!

For a moment, Darling was undecided. 'Should we tell the local cops?'

'Waste of time,' said Token. 'We still don't have a warrant.'

'Well, we can't just stand here and do nothing. I'm going up to see what I can find out. You wait here in case you get another call.' Without further hesitation, Darling began to jog up the hill towards the building. He knew he couldn't arrest Harlow but perhaps he could get a clue as to what this was all about.

His approach was obscured by tree trunks and low bushes, which allowed him to come close to the building without being observed. There was a hedge near the circular drive at the top and Darling crouched behind it. The Hilux was parked in the driveway with Harlow nowhere to be seen.

Thirty minutes later there was still no sign of Harlow and Darling was sweating profusely in the heat. Just as he decided to leave, Harlow came through the front door accompanied by a dark-skinned man with a broad face wearing a yellow shirt. They shook hands and as Harlow got into the car, Walker saw the stud in Harlow's nose flash in the sunlight. When the fellow had gone inside and Harlow had driven away, Darling retraced his steps back to the police station.

'Do you have any pictures of government officials I can look at?' he asked Token.

Twenty minutes later, after flicking through various folders, Walker found him. 'Rani Jefferson,' he read.

'Secretary for the Ministry of Petroleum.' He grimaced. 'They have a whole ministry for petrol?'

'It's one of their biggest exports since opening the fields in the western highlands,' Token said.

'What would the Ministry of Petroleum have to do with someone like Harlow?'

'You said that Runsack's brother's report had been falsified. Changed to say there was oil in the Eastern Highlands when Alf Runsack said there was none. Do you think it has something to do with that?'

Darling stroked his chin. 'Peter Runsack thought it was to do with infrastructure – roads and the like. If the oil companies thought there was oil, they'd pay for it. But surely they know they'd get caught.'

'Some people will do anything for money, even if it doesn't make sense. They think that somehow they will never get caught.'

'Maybe they won't. We don't have proof that the report was changed. All we have is the word of a dead man. The original report is gone. And I think Kronig Harlow has the only copy.'

'What now?' Token asked.

'There is someone else who can testify,' said Darling grimly.

'Who?'

'A doctor who was working with Alf Runsack just before he was murdered. Christopher Walker.' Darling paused. 'He used to be a friend of mine.'

'Used to?'

'That's a long story. But Chris Walker was a doctor working in the Eastern Highlands six years ago. He knew Runsack. And he said that Runsack told him there was no oil just before he sent his report off.'

Token frowned. 'And then Runsack disappeared. Why hasn't this Walker fellow spoken sooner?'

'He was in a bad way himself. Almost drowned in a flood. And anyway, he wouldn't have known anything about the report being changed.' Darling thought for a moment. 'Until recently, that is. Peter Runsack met with Walker and me, just before Runsack was killed. He told us about it.'

'Where is this Walker now? If he knows about the fake report, then his life may be in danger.'

'Safe and sound back in Sydney. And we know Harlow is here so unless this mob has another killer on the loose, hopefully he'll be safe.'

'Can we use him as a material witness? He's a doctor so it might stand for something.'

'Pretty weak evidence.' Darling rubbed his neck. 'I don't think it will hold up in court.'

Token sat in thought for a few moments. Then he brightened. 'What if we let it be known that there's another original report? That Alf Runsack gave it to Walker six years ago?'

'Why would we do that?'

'It would flush out Harlow. He would have to go back to Sydney and confront Walker.'

'It's dangerous. But I guess we would have Walker under surveillance and when Harlow turns up, we nab him.'

Token shrugged. 'It's the only thing I can think of. We'd watch Walker carefully so he wouldn't be in any danger.'

Darling stroked his chin in thought and stared at the photos on the desk in front of him. 'It's a plan, I suppose. We could watch Harlow from this end and follow him ourselves if he makes a move to return to Sydney.'

'We don't even have to worry Walker about it. We can nab Harlow as soon as he tries anything, and Walker need not know anything about it.'

Darling picked up the picture of Rani Jefferson. 'I can't see us getting anywhere here in PNG, especially if high-level government officials are involved. We have no power to do anything in this country except arrest Harlow. And we can't even do that, given the way they're stuffing us around.'

'What do you say then?'

Darling threw the photo back on the desk. 'Why not. Walker deserves to give something back, even if he knows nothing about it.'

Token raised his eyebrows. 'Wow. It sounds like there's a story to be told about you two.'

'I wish it was just a story. I could tell you things about him that would make your toes curl. I used to think he let his wife die, blamed him for it. Now I think that's probably not true, but there are other things.'

'Sounds like a nice bloke.'

Darling looked out of the window. 'Funny thing is, he used to be a nice bloke. Now he's just selfish. Only thinks about himself.'

Token stood up. 'Okay then. I'll get the story circulated through the local coppers that an original report still exists and that Walker has it. I'll dispatch an urgent top-secret memo back to head office in Australia.' He mimed stamping the memo with his fist. 'For "AFP eyes only".'

Darling smiled. 'So how long do you think it will take Harlow to find out?'

'About six hours.'

Darling laughed. 'What a shithole of a country.'

Token mimicked the accent of the local police. '*Mekim bisnis pasin. Kwiktaim.*' He raised his hands. 'It's the way we get things done around here.'

CHAPTER TWENTY-TWO

IT WAS 9 am the next day and Token and Darling sat together at a small cafe in the Jackson Airport terminal building, each with a cup of coffee before them. They had been waiting for an hour, making sure they got there before Kronig Harlow's expected appearance for the 9.30 am flight to Sydney.

Token, dressed in civvies, looked at his wristwatch again and nervously glanced at the main doors of the terminal. 'Where is he?' he mumbled.

'Are you sure your reports are accurate?'

'One hundred percent. He was seen to check out of his hotel at seven this morning. And I'm certain he would've got the news about Chris Walker having the report.'

Darling looked up at the flight board, which listed international and national departures – Brisbane, Cairns, Goroka, Hong Kong, Lae and others. 'The Sydney flight's on time. He's cutting it fine.'

'Here he is,' Token hissed with relief and immediately lowered his head.

Darling resisted the temptation to turn and look. After a moment, Harlow strode past carrying a sports bag and made his way to the Air Niugini counter. Darling watched as he got his ticket and noted he didn't check his bag. 'Travelling light,' he murmured to Token.

The flight to Sydney was announced and together they rose and made their way to the line that was filing out of the terminal and noted that Harlow joined the line behind them. Through the glass window, they could see the Airbus A310 parked on the tarmac, with a set of mobile stairs pushed up to the forward door.

The tropical sun had already cooked the tarmac to an unbearable temperature and the pair followed the direction of the attendant who waved them towards the line of passengers that had fanned out to trudge to the waiting aircraft. Further out, a dark-skinned lady in front bore left, and Darling went to follow her but was waved towards the right by another attendant.

'You don't want to end up in Goroka, I'm sure,' said the woman, smiling.

Darling looked to the left to see a few passengers making their way to a twin-prop plane that sat further away.

'No,' he agreed, returning her smile. 'I've been there last visit. Sydney, here I come!'

'Have a nice trip,' she called with a wave, and Darling and Token joined the group of passengers who were clustered around the base of the stairs, waiting their turn to board.

Darling glanced back in time to see Harlow coming out of the terminal building and he turned away quickly. Harlow had seen him in Sydney and Darling was worried that if he gave him too much attention, his memory might be triggered. He made a point of not looking back as he climbed the stairs and stepped onto the aircraft.

Darling and Token had seats next to each other halfway along and Token grumbled as he squeezed into the window seat. Darling surreptitiously examined every passenger who filed passed and was pleased when it eventuated that none of them were Harlow. He preferred his prey in front so it would be easy to keep an eye on him during the flight.

Token's attention was taken up with trying to fit his long legs into the narrow space, and Darling ignored him as, tutting and moaning, he twisted first one way and then the other. Darling sat up in his seat and studied the passengers in front, some still bundling their bags in the overhead lockers but most already in their seats. There was a man a few rows up who had blond hair but when he turned in profile,

Darling saw it wasn't Harlow. He ran his eyes along each row towards the front, concluding that Harlow was probably in business class, which would've also explained his late arrival at the airport.

A male flight attendant's voice came over the PA system. 'Good morning, ladies and gentlemen. All passengers are now on board and the captain has given us the go-ahead to close the cabin door. You should all now be seated with your seatbelt done up firmly across your lap. We will be away shortly.'

Still not able to see Harlow, Darling stood and opened the locker above his seat, pretending to get something from it as he carefully examined each passenger in front.

Harlow wasn't there!

'Where is he?' he hissed.

Token stopped fiddling and raised himself in his seat to peer forward. 'What?' He twisted to look behind. 'You must have missed him.'

'I didn't,' said Darling. The aisle was now clear except for a cabin attendant who was making her way towards him.

'Sir,' she said with a smile, 'can I ask you to be seated?'

'Just a sec.' He pushed past her towards the front of the cabin.

'Sir!' exclaimed the attendant. 'I must ask you to …' She paused in annoyance when Token also stood and made his way towards the back of the plane.

The PA crackled again. 'Could I ask the two gentlemen who are standing to please make their way to their seats immediately. The captain is waiting to take off.'

The two policemen met again in the middle of the aisle with the hostess wedged between them.

'See him?' asked Darling.

'Nothing. You?'

He shook his head. 'He didn't get on.' Then, with sudden realisation, he leaned over and peered out of the side window at the Dash-7 that the other passengers had been making for. Its four propellers were spinning and already the plane was taxiing to the runway. 'We got it wrong. He's going to flaming Goroka!' Darling grabbed his bag out of the still-open locker. 'Come on.'

'Sir!' exclaimed the attendant who stood between them. They ignored her as they strode to the front and the male attendant blared at them over the PA system, wide-eyed, as they stomped towards him. 'All passengers must take their seat for immediate —'

Darling cut him off by pulling the microphone out of his hand while Token, his jaws clamped tight, held his police credentials up to his face.

'OPEN THIS DOOR NOW!'

CHAPTER TWENTY-THREE

DARLING AND TOKEN checked into a guesthouse after landing at Goroka Airport at dusk the same day, having managed to secure a couple of seats on the afternoon flight out of Port Moresby. The rooms were basic but clean and the hostess was generous with her steak and chips dinner, so with their bellies full and having got over the initial shock of getting Harlow's destination wrong, they were finally able to sit back in the lounge with a beer each and reflect on where they had gone wrong.

'Why has Harlow come here, of all places?' Darling raised his eyebrows at Token. 'Obviously your clever ruse of Chris Walker having Runsack's report didn't have the desired effect.'

'Obviously,' he said, leaning back in the low lounge chair. 'But I'm not certain we made the right decision following him. We can't arrest him. We don't have a warrant.'

'We can at least see what he's up to.' He took a swig from the bottle. 'What else are we going to do? We were at a dead-end in Port Moresby. The local coppers are stalling us and some bigwig at the top of the pile is going to block anything we do. Maybe coming here at the last minute has thrown them all out.'

'Maybe,' said Token, finishing his drink. 'Let's see what tomorrow brings then, eh? But right now, I'm off to bed.'

The next morning they were out of the guesthouse by ten, deciding to make for the Goroka markets, a spot that Token guaranteed to be the site most visited by any tourists travelling to the highland town.

'He's not really a tourist,' Darling grumbled as they approached the markets across an open field.

'I can't think of anything else to do, can you?' said Token. Up ahead was a fence festooned with a myriad of coloured woven bags. 'They're called *billum*,' he said. 'The mamas here weave them. You should buy one.'

'Mamas? I thought Tok Pisin for woman was *meri*.'

'An older woman is mama. A sign of respect. I thought you were here before?'

'Only for a few weeks.' Darling waved to the women. 'Later,' he called and they smiled in return, seeming to understand him. Whether they believed him was another matter.

They spent the next two hours wandering along the rows of stalls, some no more than wares spread out neatly on blankets on the ground and others on wooden tables under timber pavilions, which provided shade and shelter from the rain.

Darling saw endless rows of sweet potatoes – or kaukau as the locals called them – as well as lettuce, cabbage and broccoli, and bright orange carrots, continually sprinkled with water to keep them fresh. In one corner were a group of stalls where cooks hunkered over fires, frying pieces of meat on metal skewers, which could be purchased for a few toya and immediately eaten.

One area was like a hardware store, with nails, padlocks, pens and pencils, forks, sunglasses and scissors spread out neatly in rows. They finally got through all the stalls but there was no sign of Harlow.

'Do you think he's left town?' asked Darling.

'Maybe,' said Token. 'No way of knowing.'

'What about the local cops?'

'I guess we could try. I wouldn't hold much hope of getting help there, if they're anything like Port Moresby.'

'Only one way to find out. Anyway, I need a break.'

The police station was a short walk away along Airport Road. They entered the two-storey concrete block building, which looked in need of a major renovation, and Token introduced them to the officer behind the counter, a young fellow with a bowl cut and beard.

'We're trying to get a message to a government contractor out of Port Moresby, a South African,' explained Token. 'The Minister for Petroleum needs to speak to him as soon as possible. He only arrived yesterday. He's easy to spot – white hair, pale skin. Has a metal stud through his nose.'

The officer said he hadn't seen him but would keep an eye out and call them at their lodgings if they found him.

'Thanks,' said Token. 'But don't tell him we're after him. He's up for an award and we want it to be a surprise.'

'Neat story,' said Darling after they left. 'Sounds like you've done that before.'

'Comes with the territory. Let's go find lunch.'

Later in the afternoon, they decided to try the markets one more time. When they got there, some of the vendors had packed up and most of the customers were tourists.

They walked past an old woman hunched over a large metal bowl set on a fire, in which sizzled a row of peeled and sliced kaukau in a pool of oil. They smelled delicious and Darling's stomach growled. He'd only had a light lunch and wondered whether he should chance it. He turned away from the vendor to ask Token his opinion but froze at something he saw at another stall further up, now obscured by the tall officer. He carefully craned his head to the side and snapped back. Kronig Harlow!

'It's him,' he hissed. 'Don't turn,' he said, when it appeared that Token was about to spin. He moved his head slowly to the side. 'He's moving. Come on.'

As they sauntered through the markets, they followed Harlow from a safe distance. Now he was walking away, Darling could safely examine him. He had white-blond hair and moved with the ease of an athlete. Or a trained soldier. Darling remembered bumping into him back in the hotel foyer in Sydney when he had to grab him to stop falling. Hard muscle, like steel. He would not be easy to arrest, even for the two of them. He had a feeling the local cops wouldn't help them either.

Harlow left the markets and walked south along the highway, crossing the road when there was a gap in the traffic. Darling and Token missed their chance to cross but were able to tail him from the other side, making sure to keep behind him. It was six fifteen according to Darling's watch, and he looked to the west to see that the sun was already setting and knew darkness would come on quickly. He gestured for Token to pick up speed. But when he looked back, Harlow was gone.

'He would've turned left at the Airport Road,' said Token.

'Come on,' said Darling, leaping out onto the road and causing a utility truck to jam on its brakes and the driver to blast his horn.

They jogged to the corner of the road they thought Harlow had taken but there was no sign of him. Off to the left was a squat building that looked like commercial premises of some sort.

'He must have gone in there,' called Darling, jogging ahead.

The security guard of the Papindo supermarket eyed them suspiciously when they jostled through the door and stopped abruptly, just in case Harlow became alerted. Token picked up a plastic shopping basket and Darling mimicked him and they walked in opposite directions to search each aisle. Darling got to the end without seeing Harlow and was about to retrace his steps when he saw his prey disappear through a rear service door, shortly followed by a young woman, one of the supermarket staff. Darling beckoned Token furiously and together they jogged out into the loading docks, just in time to see Harlow turn the corner in the direction of the main road. By the time they got back to Airport Road, Harlow was about one hundred metres ahead, barely visible in the fading light. Darling was surprised to see that the woman from the supermarket was still between them and Harlow, as if she was following him. Had Harlow partaken in a bit of shoplifting perhaps? Darling doubted it, but when Harlow crossed the road, the woman tailed him, remaining about fifty metres behind.

Harlow took an alley between two buildings and the woman increased her pace, breaking into a jog, causing Darling and Token to do the same. The sun had now set and the alley was dark, and they slowed down since they knew these rough tracks were full of potholes that could break an ankle. Soon the track opened into a field, the surrounding buildings throwing long shadows that could hold any manner of nefarious things. They ground to a sudden halt when a scream came to them from the edge of the field – a woman's.

In the darkness they crept closer and, after Darling's eyes began to adjust, he made out a group of shadows towards the edge of a building – people standing close together. They heard another muffled squeal and Darling noticed Token easing his revolver from its holster.

'What's going on there?' Darling yelled. A few of the shadows jerked towards them.

'None your *bisnis*,' came the reply, a male voice with a highland accent. '*Yu ranawe no kilim i dai pinis.*'

Darling didn't fully understand but the words were full of threat.

A woman's voice cried out, 'Please help me.' The cry terminated in an abrupt muffle as if a hand had been placed over her mouth. The accent was unmistakable.

'She's Australian,' hissed Darling over his shoulder.

'This is the police,' Token shouted, standing up to his full height and pointing his pistol with a two-handed grip. 'I have a gun. Let the girl go or I will shoot.'

A moment went by and the shadows clustered further together, as if they were conversing. Then they were gone, disappearing into the darkness like spirits. Darling and Token carefully made their way towards the area from where a quiet sob emanated.

Darling stooped down into the darkness and felt a warm body, a bare leg, then moved his arm up to her back. 'You're safe now.' She stopped sobbing. 'Can you stand?'

'I think so,' came the reply. Token moved to the other side and together they helped the woman up and supported her between them as they made their way back to the main road. Darling could feel her body trembling against his. In the light, they could see that her pants had been removed but not her underwear and top, which was torn. She had dark skin and hair, and her bottom lip was swollen and bleeding. She kept her face low but Darling thought she was the woman who'd been following Harlow.

'Do you have a hotel?' asked Token.

'My lodge is out of town.' Her voice was a hoarse whisper.

'We should take you to the police,' he said.

'No,' she rasped. 'I'll be all right. They didn't do anything serious in the end. You stopped them.'

'What happened?' asked Darling.

She rubbed her hand over her face. 'I was walking through the field when they jumped me.' She paused to let out a low sob. 'They were going to rape me.' She raised her face to him. 'Thank you.'

Now he could see her clearly in the street lamp, with a shock, Darling recognised her – the dark-skinned woman from the pub the night before Peter Runsack was murdered. 'You,' he exclaimed. 'What are you doing here?'

She bowed her head back into darkness. 'What do you mean?'

'You were in Sydney. I saw you. With another girl. Once in the Lord Nelson Pub and then the next day at the Holiday Inn. You disappeared after the murder.'

She kept her head bent. 'I don't know what you're talking about. You've got me confused with someone else.'

'Come on, Barry,' said Token. 'You can do this later. We need to get her somewhere safe.'

'The Bird of Paradise then. It's the closest hotel.'

An hour later they were seated together in the lounge of the hotel – wicker chairs and low timber coffee tables, with pot plants in the corner. The young woman was scrubbed clean from a shower and was wearing fresh clothes loaned to her by the manager's daughter. The manager had not been surprised about the attack, saying it happened all the time.

The young woman had a pot of tea before her and the two men each had a beer. They had resisted asking her any further questions and now she studied them from over a steaming cup.

'Are you both coppers then?' The tremor of her voice had gone. Her skin was clear and dark and her long brown hair was matted into dreadlocks. The blood was gone but there was a laceration on her lip and a bruise beneath it.

Token nodded and pointed his thumb at his chest. 'Australian Federal Police,' then indicated Darling, 'and New South Wales Police.'

She said nothing after that and leaned back in the chair as she sipped on her tea and stared at the faraway mountains.

'Can we ask you your name?' said Darling.

Without turning her head, her eyes flicked towards Darling and examined him for a few moments. 'Grace,' she said finally, twisting in her seat.

'Are you Australian?' asked Token and when she nodded, he continued. 'Where did you grow up?'

'Why?' She raised an eyebrow and her generous lips parted to show gleaming white teeth, although the smile was challenging rather than friendly. 'Are you going to ask me out on a date?'

Darling was intrigued. She already seemed to have recovered from her attempted rape.

'Just interested,' said Token. Then after it was clear she wouldn't say anything more, he asked, 'Are you Aboriginal?'

'Do I look it?'

'Yes,' said Darling.

She shrugged her shoulders. 'Then I am then.'

He shared a look with Token then addressed her again. 'Can I ask what you were doing in the vacant lot?'

'I was taking a shortcut back to my lodge.'

'I thought you said it was out of town.'

She paused as she stroked a finger over the bruise on her lip. 'It is. I was walking through to the next road. My friend was picking me up.'

'Friend? The blonde girl you were with? In the pub in Sydney?'

'Maybe.' She looked over Darling's shoulder to something beyond. 'Speak of the devil. Here's my lift.'

Token and Darling turned to see a slim young woman standing in the main doorway of the foyer. Her eyes ran over the two men then locked onto Grace's and her eyebrows rose questioningly. She was the opposite of her friend in appearance – white skin, straight shoulder-length blonde hair and blue eyes.

Grace rose. 'Thank you again, gentlemen. I really do owe you one.' She took a step away. 'Maybe we'll bump into each other again one day.'

But before she moved away, Darling asked, 'Why were you following Harlow?'

Grace turned and looked from Darling to Token before answering. 'I will tell you this. Be very careful with him. He is very, very dangerous. Especially in this country. He will think nothing of killing you.'

'Did you have anything to do with Peter Runsack's murder?'

'We did not,' said the white girl, who had come closer. 'And as my partner said, be careful of Harlow if you are involved with him. I warn you to keep away.'

'Is that what you two are doing?' asked Token. 'Tailing him? Or are you working with him?'

'We are most definitely not working with him,' she replied in a tight voice. 'Come, Grace, we should be going.'

Grace addressed them once more. 'Stay away from him. Leave him to us.'

After they had left, Darling took a sip of his beer then pursed his lips. 'What do you make of that?'

'Notice how the blonde girl called Grace her partner.'

'They're not police,' said Darling, matter-of-factly.

Token nodded. 'Or lesbians.'

'What then?'

Token took another sip of his beer. 'Don't know. But if we keep following Harlow, I'm sure we'll find out soon enough.'

CHAPTER TWENTY-FOUR

WALKER STRODE UP to the reception desk of the Bird of Paradise Hotel, feeling hot and bothered, having spent the day wandering around Goroka securing supplies for the trip south.

'Key for room seventeen, please,' he asked the receptionist.

All he wanted was a cold shower and he didn't even bother to look through the door into the lounge area, which he knew would be full of tourists having a drink before dinner. A nice cold beer would be lovely but it could wait.

As soon as he opened the door of his room, he knew something had been there. The cupboard doors were ajar and the contents of his backpack had been emptied onto the bed. A small folder of papers that had listed his travel plans was ripped and thrown on the ground.

Swearing, he quickly went through the items. Nothing seemed to have been stolen. As was his practice in New Guinea, he had carried his money and passport with him, leaving nothing of value in his room. But the violation was disturbing nonetheless.

He called the front desk and within minutes, the manager was in his room, apologising profusely.

'This is most uncommon,' he said. 'The *raskols* rarely break into the tourist hotels. You did the right thing taking your valuables with you. You can never be too sure.'

'No harm done, I suppose,' said Walker. 'But how could they get in? I'm sure I locked it.' He pointed to the door. 'And the lock's not broken.'

The manager bent over and squinted at the lock mechanism. 'There are scratches. Looks like someone picked the lock.' He straightened. 'Strange. The *raskols* aren't usually that sophisticated. I shall inform the police.'

'You can if you like,' said Darling. 'But leave it until tomorrow after I'm gone. Nothing's missing. I don't really want to get caught up in an investigation that's likely to go nowhere.'

'There are two Australian police having drinks in the lounge. Do you want me to ask them?'

'Really?' said Walker. He contemplated agreeing to it, more out of curiosity to see who they were. He looked at his watch. 'No, don't worry. I need to get an early start. If they're anything like the Aussie police I know, they'll want to stay up all night drinking.'

'Very well then. Will you be travelling with your South African friend?'

'South African? No, he's ...' Walker paused in thought. 'I mean yes. Yes, I will. Did he speak to you?'

'Yes, sir. Came in earlier this afternoon. Asking for you. Said he will catch up with you later. Asked me to phone him when you got back.'

Walker didn't answer. South African! Darling had said that Peter Runsack's killer was South African. But there had to be other South Africans around. 'Tell me ... my friend ... what colour was his hair?' He smiled. 'You see, I have two South African friends.'

'White. Quite distinctive.'

Walker's mind raced. This changed everything. Why would a murderer be after him? Maybe he should speak to the Australian coppers in the lounge.

The manager was speaking. 'Again, I must apologise for what's happened. The hotel will be pleased to help you in any way for the inconvenience.'

Walker made a decision. 'I've changed my plans. I'll be leaving tonight.' He moved closer to the manager and dropped his voice. 'But there's one thing you can do for me.'

CHAPTER TWENTY-FIVE

THE NEXT MORNING, the young police officer they'd spoken to the previous day phoned Token at the hotel.

'Harlow left yesterday evening after I'd finished my shift. I was only just told. Sorry for the delay.'

'Where's he gone?' asked Token.

'South. Towards Okapa. On a bike, a fast one. Trail bike.'

It took them a further two hours to hire a four-wheel drive so it had gone midday by the time they left Goroka behind.

'Twelve hours' head start,' said Darling. 'I hope you know how to drive one of these things.'

The initial journey from Goroka was along the Highlands Highway and, for the most part, the road was good. But when they turned off south at a ramshackle village, the road quickly deteriorated into a potted track that snaked its way between areas of uncleared jungle, coffee plantations and scattered shacks. To make matters worse, it started to rain.

A large truck was making its way uphill in the opposite direction and Token pulled over to let it pass. As it went by, Darling noticed the logo on the truck door. 'Chevron,' he said suspiciously. 'Just like Peter Runsack said?'

As they rounded the next bend, they could see a vehicle pulled off the road into the thick shrubs, leaving them only a narrow gap to pass.

Token jammed on the brakes. 'Stupid place to stop.'

'Looks like they've broken down,' said Darling, indicating the raised hood.

As they approached, Darling read the logo on the vehicle door. 'The Coffee Research Institute.'

Token brought their four-wheel drive to a halt and Darling leaned out of the passenger window. Two women had their heads down under the bonnet, working on the engine, their backs soaked by the constant rainfall. One looked up.

'You!' said Darling. It was the blonde girl who'd picked up Grace from the hotel the day before. A moment later, the Aboriginal woman lifted her head. She had a grease stain across her cheek and was holding a spanner, which she waved in recognition.

'Where're you headed?' she asked.

'Okapa.'

Grace looked at the other girl then back at Darling. 'Mind giving us a lift?'

'Sure,' was all Darling could think of saying. He had so many questions he didn't know where to start.

The blonde girl slammed the hood down while Grace grabbed a single overnight bag from the back seat.

'Is that all the luggage you have?' asked Darling.

'We travel light,' said the blonde as she got into the back.

'You going to leave that there?' asked Token, pointing at their vehicle.

'Can't do anything about it,' said Grace. 'It's well and truly stuffed. Someone put sugar in the tank.'

'Who would do a thing like that?' asked Darling.

'I think I have a good idea,' said Grace.

'Do you think it's our mutual friend then?' said Token.

'Who else?'

'So he knows you're after him?'

'Looks like it.'

Token eased the truck away and continued along the road towards Okapa, and Darling twisted in his seat to face the two women. 'Well, since it looks like we're travelling together, we should introduce ourselves. As we explained yesterday, this is Peter Token. He's an AFP officer working out of Port Moresby. I'm Barry Darling and I'm a detective with the New South Wales Police Service.' When neither of the women spoke, he rolled his hand in a theatrical fashion, 'And you are …?'

'I already told you,' snapped the dark woman. 'My name's Grace.'

'Grace,' said Darling. 'Is that Grace like Madonna or do you have a last name?'

'Grimes,' she said grudgingly.

'And what about you, madame?' He said the last in a fake French accent.

'Emma Spicer,' she said through tight lips.

'Great,' said Darling, putting on a smile as the truck continued to bump along the track. 'We're making progress. Now comes the hard part. What do you both actually do?'

'And don't tell us you work for the Coffee Institute,' Token chipped in.

'I don't think that's any of your business,' Emma said coolly, gazing out of the window at the jungle. Heavy rain pattered against the glass.

'Are you police?' pressed Token.

Grace let out a dismissive laugh. 'I'd hope you'd know about it if we were.'

Darling became serious. 'Listen, if we're going to help you, we need to make sure whose side you're on. As far as I'm concerned, you were seen leaving the scene of a murder in Sydney. There was a reliable witness. And I saw you the night before Runsack's murder in the pub. You were listening to our conversation. You heard what Peter Runsack said. The next day he was dead. By rights, I should arrest you.'

'You can't arrest us,' said Emma. 'You don't have the authority in PNG. You need an Australian warrant, a provisional arrest request for the local cops and extradition papers.' She gave a haughty look. 'Do you have those, officer?'

Darling made a face. 'And why would a Coffee Institute employee know that amount of legal detail? Are you lawyers?'

Emma's forehead creased and she turned back to the passing scenery.

Darling turned to Grace. 'But we all know that the killer was Kronig Harlow, don't we?' Grace also looked away, poker-faced. 'The real question is,' he persisted, 'what have you two got to do with it?' When the girls remained silent, he continued. 'Given that he tried to get you killed, Grace, I'm guessing you're not working with him. It looks like you're following him. You're clearly not police but you are Australian.'

'So?' said Emma, turning back to him. She'd regained her superior demeanour.

Walker twisted to face the front and put his head to the side. The vehicle had slowed in the heavy rain. 'You know what, Peter,' he said, ignoring his passengers in the back seat, 'I think what we have here is a pair of spooks.'

Token nodded thoughtfully. 'I think you are right, Barry.' He continued in mock realisation. 'Putting it all together, I have to agree that what we have in our back seat are a couple of ASIS agents.'

'ASIS,' repeated Darling, nodding meaningfully. 'Australian Secret Intelligence Service. Spies in other words.'

He glanced back at the two women, who were now focused on them, although they still appeared relaxed. He looked out along the dirt track before them, the wipers pumping energetically. Through the trees he could see a few huts in a small clearing, looking sad and lonely in the downpour.

'They're both young, but I suppose spies come in all shapes and sizes.'

'Good-looking too. Stand out a bit. I always thought spies should blend in with the surroundings. You know, just be as ugly as the rest of us.'

'I think it's part of their cover,' replied Darling, keeping his expression serious. 'Attractive young women in skimpy shorts. They look more like uni students, but I think it's all a disguise.'

Token glanced at his friend with a fake look of surprise. 'So, you think they're not actually eye-catching? That this is all a ruse and that underneath, they're really just two ordinary looking …'

'All right, you idiots,' interjected Grace, trying to suppress a smile. 'You can both shut up now. Just because we won't tell you who we are doesn't give you a licence to be sexist.'

'Not sexist,' said Darling, twisting again to address her. 'Factual. We are using our powers of observation to get to the bottom of it, given that you're both so tight-lipped. We can't help that the only fact we have to go on is your pleasant appearance.' He turned to Emma who had her arms crossed, also trying not to smile. 'If you had been upfront with us we wouldn't have had to stoop to such base personal detail regarding your obvious charms.'

Despite herself, Emma let out a laugh. 'I bet you say that to all the spies you meet.'

Darling smiled. 'So we *are* right. ASIS?'

Grace nodded. 'Who else? But don't think you're so clever. Given what you know, it wasn't that hard to work out.'

'If you hadn't,' agreed Emma, 'we'd question your abilities.'

'Well, since we've passed the test,' said Token, looking through the rear-view mirror, 'are you going to tell us what you're up to? Maybe we can help.'

The two young women shared a look and then Emma spoke. 'We're after Harlow. He's a nasty piece of work. He murdered Ransack, as you've worked out, but that's just the start of it.'

'Oh?' said Walker.

Between them, the young women told them what they knew about Kronig Harlow. In the 1980s, Harlow had been a Special Forces officer in the Aambeeld unit of the South African Defence Force, a unit known to carry out covert operations, which included assassinations of government opponents, and that had worked to bypass the United Nations apartheid sanctions by setting up overseas front companies.

'The unit was dissolved in '89 when the South African Border War in Angola and Namibia came to an end,' said Emma. 'Harlow, along with others of the Aambeeld unit, joined a new private enterprise called Bosses For Freedom, a UK company that offered their talents to whoever would pay.' She paused to make sure the two men followed.

'I've heard of them,' Token nodded. 'The AFP has been keeping an eye on them. They're looking to get involved with the trouble in Bougainville.'

'Already involved,' interjected Grace. 'In '89, Kronig Harlow travelled to PNG on the invitation of the commander of PNG Defence, to help with the insurrection in the copper mines on Bougainville Island. But early last year, New Guinea withdrew, leaving Bougainville under the control of the Bougainville Revolutionary Army.'

'Leaving Harlow at a loose end,' added Emma.

'That's where it gets nasty,' said Grace. 'Harlow left Bougainville and was deployed by the PNG government on a secret assignment.'

'Which is?' asked Darling.

The two women paused and, again, had a silent communication. Darling could hardly see a change in their facial expressions.

Then Grace turned back. 'Oil.'

Token and Darling exchanged a glance. 'Just as we suspected,' said Token.

'Oh?' said Grace. 'What do you suspect?'

'That there's no oil here,' said Darling.

'Not according to a government report,' countered Grace. 'The PNG government sent a geologist in the mid-80s to search for evidence of oil in the eastern highlands.'

'Don't tell me,' said Darling, raising a hand. 'The geologist's name was Alf Runsack, an Australian.'

'Correct,' said Grace.

'But Peter Runsack, Alf's brother, claimed he had a copy of the report which says there's no oil here.'

'Also correct.'

'And now both men are dead,' said Darling.

'And the report that Peter Runsack said stated there was no oil – and which contradicted the official government report that says this place is full of oil – is now gone,' concluded Grace, raising both hands.

'Harlow,' said Darling.

Both women nodded.

Token piped up. 'So now that the oil companies think there's oil down here, they're building roads and other stuff to make it possible to drill for it.'

'The oil companies will do their own investigation and pull out when no oil's found,' said Grace.

'But by then a considerable amount of infrastructure would have been built,' added Emma.

Darling said, 'So the PNG government would stoop to murder just to get a road built?'

'People have murdered for less,' said Emma. 'But we don't think it's an official government plan. We have traced it to one rogue official. We think the Prime Minister knows nothing about the lie.'

'But to prove it, we need Harlow,' said Grace.

'And the Australian government has sent you two?' Darling couldn't keep the hint of scepticism out of his voice. 'I don't mean to minimise your talents but from what you've told us, Harlow is a trained killer, and you're both ...' He hesitated.

Emma raised her eyebrows. 'Both?'

'So young,' Darling said politely.

'It's not only Harlow who has had Special Forces training, Detective Darling,' said Grace.

'You two have?' Token said with unmasked incredulity.

'Emma was top of her group and I wasn't far behind.'

Despite himself, Darling found himself staring at the women's thighs and upper arms. He had to admit, they both looked quite wiry.

'So why is Harlow travelling down here?' asked Token, now seemingly accepting of their credentials.

'Because there might be another witness. Or at least someone who can testify to the truth about Alf Runsack's original report.'

'A local then,' said Token.

Both women shook their head. 'Nope,' said Grace. 'An Australian. He was down here in '85 when Runsack was leaving the area for Moresby after he'd finished his report, just before he was killed.'

'An Australian living down here?' said Token. 'A missionary?'

'Not living. Visiting. A doctor.'

'A doctor!' said Darling. He started to have an awful feeling this discussion was not going to end well. 'An Australian doctor?'

'Yes,' said Grace. 'In fact, you know him. Christopher Walker.'

'Kit! Here? But he's in Sydney.'

'No, he's not. He left Sydney the day after you did. He's somewhere ahead of us. Left Goroka early this morning.'

Darling twisted back in his seat and stared out of the window as the truck came to a halt in a small village. Just as they stopped, the rain became torrential, rivers of water enveloping them in a silvery cocoon.

'Kit? Here in New Guinea? Bugger me!'

CHAPTER TWENTY-SIX

OKAPA WAS A sprawling collection of buildings that extended a few kilometres along a dirt track, centred around a larger collection of tin sheds and interspersed with small plots of cleared land. The rain had continued to bucket down and the track was now a small muddy river.

They started again and Grace soon pointed to a shed that was larger than others they'd passed – a green galvanised block with open windows and a veranda on one side. As they pulled up, Darling noticed a long oblong warrior shield made from curved metal leaning against one wall. On it, painted in yellow and blue, was an image of the Phantom, complete with mask and brandishing two revolvers across his chest. At the bottom, the words 'No Save Dai' had been painted in white.

'We can stay here tonight,' said Grace.

'Here?' Token said uncertainly.

'It's the Coffee Research Institute building.'

Token examined the tin shed doubtfully.

'Our cover doesn't stop at borrowing a car, you know,' said Grace. 'As far as the locals are concerned, we're from the Coffee Institute.'

'Great,' Darling said sarcastically. 'And what're you going to do when they start asking technical questions?'

Grace flung the door open and glanced back before she jumped out into the downpour. 'Answer them, of course. We both have master degrees in food technology.'

Token questioned Emma, who was poised to follow her friend. 'Really?'

'Really,' she cried, as she jumped out to follow her partner into the downpour.

'Great,' said Token to Darling. 'We're travelling with Wonder Woman and Supergirl.'

Darling turned back to look through the teeming rain at the image of the Phantom leaning against the shed wall, a pair of revolvers at the ready. "That's all we need. More superheroes.'

A minute later they were hunched together on the veranda, vainly attempting to shelter from the waterfall that was roaring off the edge of the tin roof. The door opened and they jumbled inside, dripping and squelching.

A middle-aged white man with a wide smile, beer belly and dressed in a red T-shirt greeted them, as if it was not unusual to receive visitors in such a manner.

'Caught in the bloody rain, were we?' His mouth stretched gleefully under a bushy moustache. He had an Australian accent. 'Nice and wet enough for you?'

Grace returned his smile and extended her hand. 'Lucy Carter from the Institute. I think you were expecting us. This is Mary James,' she added, indicating Emma.

'Steve Buckland, manager,' he said, shaking her hand and then Emma's. 'And you are?' he said to Darling, who remained dripping in the doorway.

For a moment, Darling wondered whether he should play the same game as the women and come up with a fake name. 'Barry ...' he said slowly, his eyes flicking to Grace.

'Darling,' she finished for him. 'And this is Peter Token. They're from the Australian police. They picked us up. Our truck broke down about twenty kilometres out of Goroka.'

'Strewth!' Steve exclaimed. 'Stone the bloody crows!' He flicked an arm into the air. Darling and Token glanced guardedly at each other. 'I've told them a million times – they've gotta take better care of those trucks. 'Specially when two women are driving alone. Bloody bastards!' He pointed at the women. 'I'm sure you girls know how to look after yourselves but you just don't know what's going to happen out here in the sticks. Why, only a couple of weeks ago, two tribes were fighting each other just like in the old days. You know, spears and shields.' He mimicked a warrior fighting with an imaginary shield and club. 'More bravado than real and no one was hurt. But some of the locals have short fuses and are just as likely to stab you as help you if they come across you alone in the bush.' He looked the two women up and down. 'Or worse, if you get my drift.'

Grace was silent for a moment, seemingly unsure of how to proceed after Steve's excited tirade. 'Thanks for your concern, Steve. Luckily, these two gentlemen happened along and –'

'Coppers, eh?' he interrupted, turning to Darling and Token. 'What brings you to these parts? Training? Mostly the Aussie cops are involved with training. Is that it?'

Darling felt it would be easier to agree but then considered it might cause problems. 'No, actually, we're following someone.'

Steve became quiet. Wary even, thought Darling.

'Following someone? May I ask who?'

'Blond hair. South African …'

'Thought so! That bastard's been in and out of here for years. Up to no good, I'm sure, although I've never been able to pin anything on him. Sneaky bastard. And dangerous by the look of him.' Steve seemed to size Darling and Token up. 'Might have your work cut out for you, if you don't mind me saying.'

'Steve,' Emma interrupted sweetly, 'do you have a place where we can freshen up?'

'Of course! Where's me manners.' He pointed to the rear of the building. 'You can both duck out the back room. There's a bathroom and a place to change.' Then he noticed their absence of luggage. 'Or not.'

The men looked at each other uncertainly after the women had left. The rain had become heavier, drumming a torrent on the metal roof, drowning out any chance of conversation. Without a word, Steve rummaged around in a corner and produced three bottles of beer and flicked off their tops. They were cold to touch and Darling savoured the feeling of it flowing down his throat. All three finished quickly and Steve produced another round. This time they sipped them more slowly.

'I saw him, you know,' offered Steve, when the beat of the downpour had lessened. 'The Saffie.' He took another sip. 'Flew through like a blue-arsed fly on a motorbike last night. Didn't stop, but I saw him as he went past.' He flicked his head sideways. 'Headed south towards Purosa.'

Soon after, Grace and Emma joined them and Steve offered them both a beer, which they accepted. The rain had settled to a steady flow and they sat on the veranda, watching the plump drops fall onto the lush lawn outside the office.

'And what about you, Lucy?' said Steve addressing Grace. 'You originally from Torres Strait?'

'I am,' said Grace, smiling. 'Most people guess that I'm Aboriginal.' She shot a meaningful glance at Token, then turned her attention back to Steve.

'I'm from the Top End,' explained Steve. 'Grew up in Darwin and Townsville. Even lived for a time on Moa Island. My father was a minister in the Methodist church and we used to move around. Which island are you from?'

'Mer.'

'Mer, eh. Same place as Eddie Mabo.'

'Not many people know that either,' answered Grace, clearly pleased.

'Causing a bit of a stir, old Eddie,' Steve said gleefully. 'I don't think he's got much of a chance though.' When he noticed that the others were looking blank-faced, he explained. 'Eddie Mabo and a few other Mer people are trying to overturn *terra nullius* – you know, that no one was here before the Europeans arrived.' When Darling and Token remained blank-faced, he added, 'So the English could claim Australia as their own. Mabo wants what they call native title to apply to Crown land. Can't see 'em winning against the greedy Queenslanders, though.'

Steve noticed that Darling and Token had switched off so he changed the subject. 'So, Lucy, I expect you've got a good set of lungs on you?' His words had the desired effect as all eyes turned to Grace.

Grace leaned back in her chair and sipped her beer. 'Not bad,' she answered, looking out into the dripping jungle. 'My uncle was a famous pearl diver and I expect I've got some of his characteristics.' She glanced at Darling, who looked away quickly. She gave a small smile then said to Steve, 'My great-grandfather was a head-hunter.'

'Are you kidding?' asked Token.

'So they say, according to the stories handed down by the Elders. May have been involved with the massacre of the crew of a boat that was shipwrecked there in the eighteen-hundreds.'

'I hope you haven't got some of his habits as well!' Steve said with a chuckle.

'You never know,' said Grace enigmatically. 'I'm pretty good with a spear, so you'd better watch out. I can spike a fish at ten metres.'

'Woo-hoo.' He chuckled, raising his palms. 'I've been duly warned.' He turned to Emma. 'And what about you, Mary? Tell us about yourself.'

Emma looked uncomfortable with the sudden interest. 'Oh, you know, normal Aussie stuff.' She took a swig from her bottle. 'Grew up in Castle Hill in Sydney. Went to Sydney Uni. That's where Lucy and I met ... doing Food Science. Worked in Sydney for a while, then we've both come up here to work with the institute.' She gave a rousing little punch of her fist. 'Get the coffee industry going and all that.'

Darling wondered how much of Emma's story was true. At least some of it, he expected, but he figured he couldn't be sure with these two. They lied too easily.

The sun had gone down and Steve looked at his watch. 'Footy's starting soon. St George versus Canterbury. Opening match of the season. Should be a good one.'

'You watch on the tele?' asked Token.

'I wish. Listen on the radio. The Sydney footy comp's pretty big up here.'

'I'm more of an AFL man,' said Token. 'Grew up in Melbourne.'

'What about you, Bazza?' asked Steve. 'You up for it?'

'Sure am,' he said, raising his bottle. 'The Berries will smash the Dragons, I reckon.'

'The Berries! Long time since I've heard that,' said Steve.

'Bulldogs, I mean,' said Darling. 'Never got used to the name change.'

'What about you girls?' asked Steve. 'In for a bit of rugby league?'

'No, thanks,' said Emma. 'We've got a few things to do and then I think we'll turn in.'

'No worries.' He pointed to a nearby raised timber building. 'Pick your own room. I use the one at the front. Loo's out the back.'

'I might hit the sack as well,' said Token. 'See you all in the morning.'

After the others had left, the two men sat sipping their beers, looking out at the rain. Steve leaned back through the open window and flipped a switch on a battered black radio that sat on a bench and a male voice blared out. Two announcers were talking about the upcoming match, so he turned the volume down.

Darling pointed with his beer at the Phantom shield, which sat facing them on the wall of the hut opposite. 'What's the shield for? Did someone leave it?'

'I collect them. Might be worth something one day. I bought that one off a fellow from the other village who took part in the brouhaha the other day. Says it belonged to his father. I reckon it was done in the seventies. A classic.'

'Is the Phantom common?'

'Yea. Big following round here. I think it's something about how the Ghost Who Walks lives with the blacks – protecting them, – being on their side. I think that attracts them, even though the real Phantom is somewhere in Africa.'

'Real Phantom?'

'Well, the original one, at least.'

Darling studied the image again. It was crudely painted but the blue-purple of the Phantom's suit on the stark yellow background was captivating, and the muscular arms, which brandished a pair of black revolvers, gave it a menacing air. 'What do the words mean? *"No Save Dai"*?'

'Not sure. I think it means "will not die". I speak Tok Pisin but I forgot to ask the fellow. Context is everything.'

Darling was silent for a few moments as he contemplated the image. 'You know, I used to be in the Phantom Club.'

Steve twisted in his seat. He extended his beer bottle and touched Darling's in a salute. 'You don't say. A fellow Phantom Phreak, hey?'

'You too?'

'Still am. It's very strong in PNG. I've still got my rings.'

'Really? Truth be told, so do I. I even brought them. A few of the coppers in Mount Hagen were Phreaks so I thought I'd better show solidarity if I bumped into them again.'

'That doesn't surprise me. The coppers here are especially into the Phantom – silent strength, getting the bad guy and all that.'

'"Nobody argues with the Phantom and wins",' recited Darling.

'"Never point a gun at the Phantom",' replied Steve with a smile.

Darling paused in thought, then said, '"When the Phantom asks, you answer".'

Steve replied immediately. '"No man can refuse the voice of the Phantom".'

Darling let out an exasperated breath and gritted his teeth as he searched his memory while Steve's grin slowly widened. Finally, Darling gave a triumphant murmur. '"The voice of the angry Phantom freezes a tiger's blood".'

'"Better to stare into the tiger's eyes than into the cold eyes of the angry Phantom",' countered Steve without pause.

Darling gave a defeated moan then laughed. 'All right, you win.'

'Never been beaten,' Steve said with a satisfied look. 'You did well though.' He tipped his beer against Darling's again. 'On to even more important things,' he said, as he reached back through the window and turned up the radio. 'The footy.'

The air became filled with the sound of cheering fans overlaid with the voice of an excited announcer, and the two men leaned back in their chairs just as the downpour started up again, a crate of beer between them.

Early the next day, Darling was woken by a shake on his shoulder. Token was standing over him. 'They're gone.'

He moaned. 'What?' he mumbled, opening his eyes a slit then closing them shut again.

'Emma and Grace. They've cleared off. And they've taken the car.'

Darling sat bolt upright, then grimaced and cradled his head in his hands. 'The car?' he croaked. 'You sure?'

He stumbled outside, blinking, with Token close behind. The four-wheel drive was nowhere to be seen.

'Bugger me!' said Darling, one hand on his forehead and the other on his hip. He stared down the dirt road. 'I didn't see that coming.'

CHAPTER TWENTY-SEVEN

CHRISTOPHER WALKER AND Justin Namah had arrived at Purosa, a small village south of Okapa, the evening before, after a demanding drive along tracks thick with mud. With the scare in the hotel, Walker had spent the night at Justin's and they'd left Goroka early in the morning. He only hoped the ruse he'd set up had worked. He'd asked the manager to contact the South African to inform him that Walker had left Goroka in a hurry that night, travelling south towards the Fore villages. If the story had worked, the Saffie would be somewhere ahead of them.

Approaching Purosa, they'd been bogged twice on slippery slopes but had managed to get through with the help of locals, who'd joined together to push the back of their truck. They'd driven through Okapa at lunchtime just as the rain started; it had lasted all afternoon and now effectively ended any chance of driving further. Even in the best weather, the track south of Purosa was difficult by four-wheel drive and would now be impossible. From here, Walker realised, they'd have to travel on foot.

They spent the night with an old friend, the leader of the village – a thin, middle-aged fellow who they'd met on their previous journeys years before. He still wore the same baseball cap and ACDC T-shirt that Walker recalled from that time. Many of the villagers recognised them from their work with the TB medical team six years ago and Walker and

Justin spent the evening catching up. There was a burgeoning coffee industry but it was clear the villagers were struggling. Most had their own coffee plots and there was no shortage of seed or land. The main problem was transport of the beans to the factory, which was all the way up at Goroka, an impossible distance for the local farmers.

'But we have been promised a road,' said the leader. 'A foreigner came. He is working with the government for a long time. He was here years ago but has come back to tell us it will come here soon. Then we will be able to get our crops to the factory. It will be very good for us.'

'A foreigner?' said Justin. 'Is he still here?'

'No, he left a few hours ago. On a motorbike.' The fellow pointed south, the direction Walker and Namah were about to take. 'You must know him,' he added, pointing to Walker. 'But he's not Australian.'

'Know him? Why would I know him?'

'He asked for you. Christopher Walker.'

Walker and Justin shared a look. 'What does he look like?' asked Justin.

'Tall,' said the man. Then he ran a hand over his head. 'Hair white.'

'Do you know him?' Namah asked Walker.

He shook his head slowly. 'No. But if it's the same fellow who searched my room, I know who he is.' He addressed the villager. 'You say he was here years ago? Was it at the same time as me?'

The man lifted his arms. 'Maybe.'

'Has he been coming and going over these last few years or has he just come back?'

'Just now,' was the answer. 'Yesterday. He wanted to know if Christopher Walker had come through and we said no. We said you were here six years ago but not since.'

'If he wants to speak to me, why didn't he wait for us?'

'He said you might be going another way. But he said he knew where you were going.'

'Knew where I'm going? How could he?'

The village leader shook his head. 'Don't know. But he promised us a road. We are very happy.'

They spent the next morning checking their backpacks and buying food from the villagers and generally getting ready for what would be a five-day trek through the highland jungle. They were finally ready to go, later than Walker had hoped, and a few of the villagers gathered to farewell them. The deluge had not let up overnight and they were surprised when they heard a vehicle travelling towards them along the Okapa road. Walker thought the track would be unpassable with all the rain overnight, given the difficulty they'd had the previous day.

They stood together with the villagers in the clearing and watched as a Landcruiser approach. At the wheel, Walker was surprised to see a young black woman, a local by the looks of her. In the passenger seat was her opposite in appearance – a blonde woman with pale skin. Walker couldn't remember ever seeing a local woman driving a four-wheel drive in the highlands. The vehicle was parked and the two women got out and gave a wave. Walker and Justin watched curiously and waited for the women to reach them.

'Road's a mess,' said the dark woman. She had an Australian accent.

'I'm surprised you made it through,' said Justin.

'Used to it,' replied the dark girl. She looked around as if she was searching for someone. The blonde was doing the same. To Walker they appeared cautious, but not about the local villagers, which he would've expected from two women travelling alone. And they looked familiar somehow ...

'We work for the Coffee Research Institute,' said the blonde, her eyes still roving.

'You both sound Australian,' said Walker.

'We are,' she said.

'I was a bit surprised,' said Walker. 'I thought you were a local,' he added, indicating the dark woman.

'Common mistake,' she said, her attention finally resting on Walker. She offered her hand for him to shake. 'Lucy Carter. This is Mary James. As Mary said, we work for the Coffee Research Institute. And you are?'

'Chris Walker. And this is Justin Namah.' He noticed Mary was again studying the village. 'You two appear to be looking for someone.'

'We are,' said Mary, her eyes flicking back to Walker. 'A South African. Works for the government. White-blond hair.'

Walker grimaced and shook his head. 'Haven't seen him.' There was something about the two women. Shifty. He didn't want to give them anything. Then he remembered; her asking about the South African had triggered his memory. They were the two women in the Lord Nelson, the ones he'd seen running near the murder scene.

The one called Lucy Carter pointed to his backpack. 'Going for a walk?'

'Thinking of it,' said Walker. He looked at the girls closely. 'Have we met before?'

'I don't think so,' said Lucy quickly.

'You both seem so familiar,' he insisted. 'Maybe you were working in the area six years ago when I was here?'

The dark girl shook her head and half-turned away. The blonde turned completely and went back to surveying the village.

'No, we weren't in PNG six years ago,' said the dark woman. 'You must be mistaking us for someone else.'

'Maybe.'

'When will you be heading off?' asked the blonde, without turning. 'You'd better not leave it too late. Don't want to get caught out after dark.'

'Soon,' said Justin. 'But hey, I sometimes go to the Agricultural Research Station at Aiyrua. Do you know it?'

'Yes,' said Mary. 'It's just down the road from the Coffee Institute.'

'You must know James Ireland then.'

Mary paused for a moment then got a look of recognition. 'Oh yes …'

'No, I'm pretty sure we don't know him,' Lucy interrupted firmly. 'We're not there that much. We're mostly on the road doing this sort of thing.'

There was an uncomfortable pause while the two men looked from one woman to the other, expecting more. When it was clear that neither would say anything else, Walker asked, 'Isn't it dangerous for two women to be travelling around the highlands by yourselves?'

'We know how to look after ourselves,' said Lucy.

'We cover each other's back,' added Mary.

'I wouldn't have thought the institute would allow you to travel without protection,' said Walker.

'Why?' said Lucy shortly. 'I don't see you two with a bodyguard.'

Walker didn't reply.

'Where are you two off to anyway?' Mary asked brightly, changing the mood.

Justin pointed to the rough walking track that led south away from the village. 'Urai. It's about a day's walk.'

'That's out of the way,' said Lucy. 'What are you up to down there?'

Walker butted in. 'Justin and I used to work around here years ago with the TB team.'

'Very noble of you,' said Mary.

'Not really. Anyway, we're visiting one of the villages to see how they're going.'

'Long way to come for a friendly visit,' said Lucy.

'Well, we were down this way so we thought we should look in.'

'Oh? What brings you to PNG?' asked Mary.

Walker decided to shut them down. 'If you must know, my wife died here six years ago.' He tried to make his voice rough. 'I'm revisiting the area. I want to check a few things out. Put her spirit to rest.'

There followed a tense silence. Walker was used to people being shocked and uncomfortable when he spoke of his wife's death but instead, he saw interest and wariness in the girls' faces. It was as if they already knew about Felicity.

'That's very sad,' said Lucy, although there was no empathy in her voice.

'How did she die?' asked Mary.

'Does it matter?'

'Just asking,' said Mary.

'Anyway, we'd better get going,' he said, turning away and pulling his backpack onto his shoulders. 'We want to get to Urai before nightfall and it's a bit of a walk.'

The two men walked away along the track and when Walker looked back, the women were still standing where they'd left them, silently staring.

They didn't wave.

Walker and Justin trudged along a muddy trail that gradually sloped downwards through thick jungle, dripping with rain. Walker had set a fast pace and, after a kilometre, Justin called out for him to slow down.

Walker stopped on the track just before it plunged downwards into a valley, the rocky way broken up by small rushing rivulets from the rain.

'I wanted to get a bit of space between us and those women,' he said when Justin reached him, puffing and sweating despite the rain. 'I realise who they are. It took me a while to place them out of context. They were in a pub in Sydney the night before Peter Runsack was murdered. And I saw them both leaving the murder scene.'

'Peter Runsack? Murdered?'

'Alf's brother. It happened a few weeks ago.'

'And who's this white-haired fellow in front of us? The South African? Is he the one asking questions about you at the Bird of Paradise?'

     Howard Gurney

'Probably. There was a blond chap in the same pub as the two women and a white-haired man was witnessed strangling Peter Runsack. Maybe they're in cahoots. And I remember my policeman friend, Barry Darling, saying something about him being South African.'

'What's this all about, Chris? You didn't tell me about a murder. I thought this was about Felicity.'

He chewed his bottom lip. 'I don't know what it's all about or whether Alf's death had anything to do with Felicity. I can't see how it could have. She drowned. But Peter Runsack's murder puts everything into a different light. The South African.' He pointed up the trail. 'Those two girls. I don't know what to make of it.'

'Sounds menacing.'

'I agree.'

'You sure they were the girls you saw in Sydney?'

'Positive. I don't know what their role is in all this but I wouldn't trust them as far as I can throw them.'

'So, this South African ahead of us, is he dangerous?'

'He could be a murderer.'

'Why's he promising roads to the locals then? Saying he's working with the government. Maybe that's true, maybe it's not, but it's all very suspicious.'

'Alf Runsack had written a report that said there was no oil down here. But the government's copy of the same report said the opposite. If there was oil down here then companies would be falling over themselves to be involved in exploration.'

'And building roads,' said Justin.

'And building roads,' repeated Walker. He looked out over the treetops. 'Maybe we've bitten off more than we can chew.' He gazed back up the trail. 'But those women are behind us. And they could be murderers too. I vote we keep going.'

'Count me in,' Justin answered.

A Toyota Hilux, Steve Buckland at the wheel, came screaming and slipping along the last muddy stretch of the road that led from Okapa to Purosa and pulled up in the village clearing. Grace and Emma, who'd gathered a stack of fruit and vegetables around them, watched as the vehicle approached. Darling glared at them from the passenger seat while Peter Token was already out of the truck coming towards them.

'What do you think you two are up to?' Token shouted before he reached them. 'Do you realise we can have you for –'

'It's safer this way, Peter,' interrupted Emma. 'We told you before, Harlow's dangerous. He's a killer. It's better that you leave him to us.'

'Who do you bloody well think we are? I'm a trained Australian Federal policeman.' He jerked his thumb over his shoulder. 'Barry's a detective in the New South Wales Police Service, for heaven's sake –'

'And Kronig Harlow is an assassin and Special Forces trained. No insult intended but you don't have the skills.'

Darling, who had got out of the car, exploded. 'And you do?'

Grace said, 'Yes, we do. We're better equipped to deal with him.'

'Bullshit!' he said. 'I've come here to arrest him and that's just what I'm going to do.'

'You won't arrest him,' Grace said calmly. 'He'll either kill you or you'll have to kill him. Nothing less.' She stared into Darling's eyes. 'Can you do that? Kill a man?'

He hesitated and licked his lips. 'If I need to,' he said, his voice uncertain. 'Are you sure he's ahead?'

Grace nodded. 'Yes, he came through yesterday. And what's more, your friend Chris Walker left to follow him less than three hours ago.'

'Chris! Are you sure?'

'The village leader knows him from when he was here six years ago. When Walker's wife drowned.'

'You know about that?'

'We think that's why Harlow is here. He's worried that Walker knows about the fake report.'

Darling looked guiltily at Token. 'It's worse than that. He thinks Walker has a copy of the original report with him.'

'Oh?' said Grace. 'And has he?'

'No. But we spread a rumour back in Port Moresby that he did.'

Emma remained calm. 'And why would you do a dumb thing like that?'

'We thought Walker was in Sydney. We were trying to draw Harlow back to Australia so we could nab him.'

'That clearly didn't work,' said Grace.

Darling looked south along the trail that Walker must have taken. 'What do you think Harlow will do when he finds him?'

'See if he does have a copy,' said Grace.

'And when he finds he doesn't?' said Darling.

'Kill him,' said Emma.

CHAPTER TWENTY-EIGHT

WALKER AND JUSTIN reached Urai just as the sun was setting, after a hard day's walk. The track had been longer and more difficult than Walker remembered, through thick jungle, along thin footpads atop mountain ridges, then steep descents to cross flimsy bridges thrown across rushing streams. The rain had been relentless and they were soaked through.

The village had changed little in the six years since they'd been there, the last village they'd visited before that fateful day when Felicity had died. The settlement was a loose collection of a half-dozen raised, circular huts constructed of grass walls and thatched roofs, and as they approached, a man who had been digging in a patch of muddy dirt straightened and examined them closely. White visitors were no longer a novelty but the village was far enough away from civilisation for a visit from a white stranger to warrant attention. The man threw down his shovel then bent over and picked up a large machete and walked towards them, wiping the dirt from his free hand on his trousers. When he drew closer, Walker realised he knew him.

Walker stopped and called out to him, unsure of the reception he'd receive. 'Vincent! Don't you remember us?' Walker gestured to his friend. 'You remember Justin? And I'm Christopher Walker. We did the TB clinic with you.'

The man frowned but continued to approach them and stopped a few steps away. His frowned deepened as he examined Walker's face carefully, ignoring Justin.

'You are dead,' said the man. He was muscular, with a well-defined nose and strong face.

Walker raised his arms and gave an unsteady smile. 'Obviously not.'

Vincent looked uneasily over his shoulder towards the village then back again, still frowning. 'You sure? I'm pretty sure you're dead.' He peered suspiciously to one side then the other, then addressed Walker again. 'Maybe you're a spirit.'

Justin took a step backwards and held Walker's sleeve in warning. It had been common practice for highlanders to kill strangers on suspicion of being spirits or sorcerers. 'I think we'd better go,' he hissed.

Vincent looked acutely from Justin to Walker, slapping the blade of the machete menacingly in his free hand. But then he broke into a wide smile and began to chuckle, quickly metamorphosing into a mighty guffaw, slapping his thighs with mirth. 'Got you!' he shouted with glee. 'You thought I was going to conk you on the head with my sword, didn't ya? Ha ha ha!' He threw the machete on the ground then grabbed Walker in a hug. 'Good to see you, old friend.' Still hugging Walker's shoulder, he shook his companion's hand. 'And you too, Justin. It has been a long time.'

'Six years,' said Walker, smiling. 'Too long.'

Vincent released his hold and took on a morose appearance. 'But your wife, Flea. I think it is true that she has gone. We had news.'

He nodded. 'Yes, that is true.'

'News is, she was drowned in a flood.' Vincent had become careful, questioning.

'That's what we thought at the time,' said Walker with equal care.

'Do you still think it?'

'A friend of mine came here. A policeman from Australia. He told me he found the hut where I'd been kept after I'd almost drowned. He said he found Felicity's bones.' Walker pursed his lips before he continued. 'Reckons her skull had been cracked open.'

Vincent drew himself up and nodded slowly, taking a deep breath. 'Cracked open?' His face was bland, giving nothing away. 'You know that our Elders used to honour our dead by feasting on them? It would allow their spirit to return to the land of our ancestors. Our women would do that honour.' He was silent as he examined Walker and then Justin. When they said nothing, he continued. 'An old woman cared for you. A woman from another tribe.'

'That's why we have returned,' said Walker. 'I need to find out if that's what happened. Or … whether something else happened.'

'Something else?'

Walker thought it curious that Vincent wasn't surprised.

'Vincent, it's possible that Flea didn't drown.'

Vincent looked back at the village then pointed along the track in the other direction. 'Come with me. It's best we talk alone.'

He led them down a steep incline until they reached a clearing surrounded by thick vegetation where he stopped. 'News of the bones being found reached us. We know about it. It has caused problems.'

'What sort of problems?'

'Problems about the other Australian. He was here in the village the day you left.'

'Alf Runsack? The geologist? What about him?'

'We think he was killed.'

'How do you know?'

Vincent shook his head. 'Don't know, just think. The same day you went north, he left for Purosa. He said he had a report for the government. We didn't think anything of it. Strangers were always doing reports for the government. It had nothing to do with us. Nothing ever changed for us.'

'So why do you think he was killed?'

'That same day, bad men came. Men from another village. Weya. Not our *wantok*.'

'How do you know they were bad?'

'We are not friends since my grandfather's time. They stole from us. We fight them. A long time ago, wars. We killed many of their *wantok*. We are careful of them. They would kill us but we are too strong. They will steal our pigs or women if we do not watch out.'

'Did you see them do something to Alf Runsack?'

'No. But they came close to our village. We saw them pass. They went the same way as Runsack.'

'Hmm,' said Walker. It sounded suspicious but he knew it proved nothing.

'But there was someone else with them,' continued Vincent. '*Waitpela*. White man. A man with hair like clouds.' Vincent waved his hands around his own head. '*Wait gras*. White, white.'

Walker turned to Justin. 'The South African.'

'And another thing,' added Vincent. 'He's back.'

'White hair? Here now?'

'Yesterday. I saw him.'

'What does he want?'

'He said you might come here. Wants us to tell him if you come.'

'Are you sure it was me he was after?'

'Christopher Walker,' he said. 'Doctor.'

Walker gritted his teeth and nodded. 'Yes, they said the same in Purosa. Said he was looking for me.'

'He said he had news about your wife. Said he wanted to speak to you about her.'

'Felicity? What would he know about her?'

'Don't know, Chris,' said the highlander, shaking his head. 'But be careful. He's dangerous, big time.'

'Where's he now?' asked Justin.

Vincent waved his arm westward. 'Gone to the other village. To see Weyamen.'

Walker stared into the dense jungle to the west. 'That's where we're going,' he said. 'Where Felicity died. Where her bones were buried.'

'*Ples nogut*,' said Vincent, shaking his head. Such was his anxiety, he had broken into Tok Pisin. '*Man tru nogut*. White-haired man very bad. Weyaman *nogut*.'

Walker turned to him. 'Vincent, I must go. I need to find out what really happened to Flea.' Then he addressed his companion. 'But, Justin, I can't ask you to come. It sounds too dangerous.'

He shrugged his broad shoulders and his lips parted in a smile, showing white teeth. 'It's not the first time I've been in danger in the highlands, Chris. We'll just have to be careful.'

As he finished speaking, the rain abruptly stopped and the sun shone down through a break in the clouds. The three men looked up.

Walker let out a restrained laugh. 'Shall we take that as a sign?'

'I guess so,' said Justin.

'Okay,' said Walker. 'First thing in the morning. Vincent, can we depend on your hospitality?' As he spoke he reached into this backpack and pulled out a handful of kaukau, which he'd purchased that morning from Purosa.

Vincent bowed his head and waved his arm back towards the grass huts of the village. 'Welcome, welcome. Come, we will eat.'

The rain had started again during the night and by daybreak it had become torrential. Undeterred, Walker and Justin set out early after a cold breakfast of leftovers from the evening before, waving their thanks to the villagers who'd harboured them.

The track followed a ridge at times, and at other times dived steeply towards the valley floor far below, where it became no more than a rivulet of mud and water. More than once, Walker slipped on rocks and soil that came away under his feet. Soon he was a muddy mess, although the relentless downpour quickly washed away most of the muck from his upper body.

They were soaked to the skin and Walker was glad he'd thought to cover his Berghaus with a garbage bag, which he'd packed for that purpose. He'd been caught before with a backpack full of water and sodden food and clothes, all rendered worse than useless and weighing a ton.

By midmorning, they reached a cliff face close to the bottom of the valley, which overlooked a rushing stream that wound through a rocky gully. The track followed the top of the cliff but in places the track disappeared, having been washed away by the rain, and they had to climb up into the thick jungle to continue. Eventually, Walker spied what he was searching for, – a rope bridge that spanned the stream to the cliff on the other side. Three lengths of cable made up the rudimentary bridge – two used as handrails, leaving the third as a footpath on which to walk, the whole structure supported by an intricate weave of rope on each side.

Justin went first as Walker used his weight to vainly try to stabilise it, while his friend made his precarious way across, the whole bridge swaying violently from side to side. Walker followed confidently, having crossed such bridges on many occasions six years before, but he lost his footing when the structure jerked halfway across. One leg slipped off towards the rocks below and his other cramped painfully beneath him. He pulled a muscle in his shoulders and for a moment thought he'd have to let go. But he managed to hold on. Painfully, he pulled himself up and was able to get his boot back on the flimsy bridge, then clung on tightly while he waited for the swinging to subside, the rope digging into his palms. He contemplated jettisoning his backpack, but after a few deep breaths, he pushed on until finally he collapsed on the track at the other side.

'That was a lot of fun,' he gasped, while Justin leaned over him, grinning widely.

'Thought you were going for a swim for a second. You okay?'

'Will be. Just need a moment.' He looked down at the crashing river below. 'Seems harder than before.' Walker thought back to a month ago when he'd experienced a clumsy hand. That had disappeared and the power in his arms and legs now felt normal. The double vision had also gone. He doubted he would have made it if he still had that. He pushed the memory from his mind. He didn't want to think of what might have caused it – whether it would return. Whether it would progressively worsen until he was no more than a vegetable.

'You're six years older, Chris. You're practically an old man.'

'Thanks, Justin. But the same goes for you, you know.'

'Oh no, I'm a native.' He laughed. 'We stay in peak condition right up until we die at a premature age from some sort of preventable disease or a violent accident.'

Walker gave a laugh, although he realised his friend was speaking the truth. He remained sitting on the ground. 'Justin, have you ever seen a case of kuru?'

'Kuru?' He shook his head. 'Died out years ago. Used to be a lot around here but it's gone now that cannibalism has been stamped out. I've heard a lot about it, though.'

'How does it normally start?'

'Starts slowly with headaches and shakes. Unsteady walking – like they're drunk. Then they progressively get worse. Memory goes – you know, like they're demented. Can't walk or eat. Then they die.' Justin looked down at his friend with a curious expression. 'Why do you ask?' Then he laughed. 'Do you think you've caught it?'

Walker gave an empty laugh in return. 'No. No.' He looked away. 'How could I have got it?'

Justin laughed again. 'By eating someone's brains.' His smile was wide. 'Do any of that when you were last here?'

Walker pushed himself to his feet. 'Don't be stupid,' he snapped. 'Why would I do that?'

Justin clearly sensed the seriousness in Walker's reply and his smile abruptly vanished. 'Only joking, Chris. Are you okay?'

'Never felt better.' He heaved his pack onto his back. 'We'd better get going.'

Soon they were puffing and sweating up the next steep incline and Walker was glad of the rain, since it cooled him off, although it made the track treacherous. They continued in the same way for most of the day, climbing up and descending two more mountains, leaving them both completely exhausted. They had stopped for lunch in a clearing on one of the peaks where an abandoned hut was perched, a skeleton of timber poles that could easily be reinstated using bundled grass after the soil had finally recovered from the previous crops.

Walker stared across at the next mountain and he convinced himself he could see a collection of a few huts. 'Do you think we could bypass Weya?' he asked, knowing what the answer would be.

'No. This is the only track. If we try to make our own way, we'll get lost. Besides, I doubt there's another way. We would have to follow the river at the bottom and we'd end up too far south, past the edge of nowhere. There aren't even any villages down there and we'd starve.'

'Weya it is then.'

Towards the end of the day, feeling soaked and sorry for themselves, the two men climbed the final rise towards the small village of Weya. A mangy dog picked up their scent before the huts came into view and it stood on the track barring their way, barking loudly until a group of men arrived, who clustered behind the dog, talking among themselves.

Finally, a stringy fellow wearing a T-shirt and jeans detached from the group and walked towards them. His gums were red from chewed betel nut and he spat out a congealed lump onto the track before them.

'Where you from?' he asked roughly, a superfluous question in Walker's opinion given that there was only one track.

Walker stretched his mouth into what he hoped was a smile. 'We are heading to Misapi Mission.'

'From Australia then,' said the man, answering his own question. His smile was a ghastly sight of stained teeth and bright red gums. He waved his hand. 'Come, come. You come.' He examined Justin briefly then seemed to dismiss him.

Silently, they walked the last portion of the track, closely surrounded by the men, with the mangy dog trailing behind.

The village was a cluster of grass huts of differing size, which surrounded a central clearing that had been rendered a muddy pool by the incessant torrent of the last few days. There was no sign of vehicles or any other forms of modernisation, which Walker was used to seeing even in the most primitive villages – no TV antennae or electricity wires, no satellite dishes or petrol chainsaws – just a sad cluster of men and a few old women who examined them suspiciously as the procession arrived.

Walker was startled to see one man standing separate from the rest, whose appearance, at first, made no sense. He knew it had to be the man they had been following – white-blond hair and fair skin. A silver stud was stuck through the septum of his nose just above his lip. Walker recalled that Ali Harb had said that Peter Runsack's killer had a metal stud. But he was bare-chested and wearing a grass skirt, and the upper part of his face was painted yellow and his lips outlined in blood-red.

The man raised an arm and smiled. 'Welcome!' He came towards them. 'My name is Kronig Harlow.' He had a South African accent. 'You have excellent timing. You got here just as the ceremony is about to start.'

'Ceremony?' said Walker, frowning in puzzlement.

'My final initiation ceremony.' Harlow puffed out his chest proudly. 'After tonight I will be a proper Weyaman.'

Walker looked around. It seemed absurd. 'You've come here for a ceremony?'

'What else?' he said. Walker had to admit he had a look of excited anticipation about him, like a teenager about to go to his first formal. 'This is the final stage.'

'And that's why you're here?'

Harlow smiled amiably. 'Of course. This is a long way to come for a walk.'

'But why were you asking about me?'

He looked puzzled. 'Asking about you?' He frowned then switched to a look of understanding. 'You must be Chris Walker.'

Walker stiffened. 'Yes. What do you want of me?'

'I heard you were travelling down here.' His voice softened. 'I know something about your poor wife.'

'My wife? What could you possibly know?'

'About her death.' Harlow looked around at the villagers, who were all watching their interaction intently. 'But not now. Later. When we are alone.' He stepped away and gestured. 'You will stay tonight? It would be an honour to have you witness me being accepted fully into the tribe.'

Walker glanced around at the meagre huts and poorly dressed villagers and wondered why the man would bother. He examined the man before him again. He was unarmed but that didn't make Walker feel any safer. He had strangled Peter Runsack with his bare hands. But he knew he had no choice. He couldn't go on – it was a day's journey to the next village. They couldn't go back either. He realised the safest place was right here where he could keep an eye on Harlow.

'Of course,' he said. 'It is us who are honoured.'

CHAPTER TWENTY-NINE

DARKNESS CAME AND the thumping started, a muted beat that shook the ground and bounced off the grass walls of the surrounding huts before escaping into the misty air of the mountain top. The rain had come again but now had settled to a constant drizzle, and Walker and Justin sat cross-legged before a large fire that had been lit on a dry patch of ground on the edge of the village, their backs chilled as they slowly became soaked, their fronts warm and dry from the blazing flames.

Figures swayed off to one side, ghastly painted faces with crazy feathered heads and painted limbs with bare bellies, like medieval monsters from a storybook. A mesmerising chant came from the huddle, high and low, strangely blended and haunting.

The pair waited nervously, sipping carefully on an alcoholic brew that had been offered to them. Walker knew he couldn't trust the man. He was a murderer. But in this one thing – this ceremony – he seemed genuine. If he meant harm to him or Justin, he doubted he would've gone to such an elaborate ruse. But they would have to be careful.

Then Harlow appeared, naked except for an extravagant headpiece of feathers and wood made to resemble a bird of prey. The silver stud through his nose was replaced with a piece of bone, tapered at both ends. By now the pyre was tall and quavering, and embers flittered up into the jungle like fireflies dancing. Now the old men of the village moved towards the flame, then one after another jumped inwards to kick at the burning wood, spreading it across the ground, sending a swirling spray of red cinders into the air.

Harlow moved forward to the edge of the fire, then, after a short pause, walked to the middle of the carpet of hot coals that had been formed. He paused in the centre and turned to the others, the flames rising behind him. The beat of wood-on-wood continued, louder and faster, while the chanting broke into a delirious cacophony. Harlow's face was in shadow but Walker caught the agony on his face. Finally, when the torment had reached an intolerable crescendo, the initiate jumped away from the flames and, with a shout, ran from the clearing into the safety of the wet jungle.

The beat continued, slowing, becoming softer, while the men continued their chant, which again became blended and melodious. The singing went on for some time and Harlow did not return.

Finally, the ceremony wound down. The beating stopped and the old men in feathers retreated into the jungle. An old woman gestured for Walker and Justin to follow and showed them into one of the huts. For a while, Walker stood watching from the doorway of the hut but Harlow was nowhere to be seen. Sometime in the night Walker fell into a fitful sleep. In his dreams, the Phantom came, standing on the edge of the village to watch over them, his arms folded across a purple chest, eyes masked and face proudly steadfast.

The next morning, Walker woke to the sound of someone nearby heaving up the contents of their stomach. His next thought was the realisation that he was in one piece. Harlow had not come at them in the night.

He rolled over and sat up, peering through the door of the hut. Torrential rain still poured down into the jungle beyond the hut. But closer, Walker could see the shadowed outline of his friend filling the doorway, leaning forward on all fours and vomiting noisily onto the dirt outside.

'You okay, Justin?'

After a few more heaves, he sat back on his heels. 'Food poisoning,' he groaned. 'I feel terrible.'

Walker pushed himself to his feet and stood unsteadily for a few seconds. Maybe they'd drunk more grog than he'd realised, or maybe they'd put something into the drink other than alcohol. He kneeled and rummaged through his Berghaus and finally found what he was looking for. A water bottle.

He walked on his knees to his friend and offered the flask. 'It's good. From the last stream we crossed.'

Justin nodded and took a swig. He grimaced but managed to keep it down. Walker helped him back into the hut and onto the dry grass that was their bed.

'You stay here. Drink if you can. We're not going anywhere today.' He looked out through the door. 'Besides, it's still pissing down. Does it ever stop? I can't remember this much rain.' He glanced down at his friend, who'd said nothing. Justin's eyes were closed and he was breathing deeply. Maybe he'd been up longer than Walker had realised. Probably didn't get much sleep.

Sighing, he looked out into the gloomy torrent. He couldn't see a soul. He was hungry. What was he going to do for breakfast? He couldn't smell anything cooking. His stomach growled. He looked back down at his friend who was fast asleep.

'Only one way to find out,' he proclaimed to no one but himself.

Walker stepped out into the downpour, wincing, but then relaxing as he became soaked. He couldn't do anything about it. And it wasn't cold rain, just wet. 'Come on, you big baby,' he muttered to himself. His dream from the night before came into his mind – a purple-garbed and masked figure standing guard over the village. *What would the Phantom do right now?* He straightened his back and clenched his fists. *He'd just push through.* He raised his face to the sky and let the water wash over him. *And he'd bring the murderer to justice.* He shook his face and hair and felt the water spray away but let the rest dribble down under his clothes, resisting the temptation to pat his collar down. He knew he had no chance of fighting Harlow. But he couldn't run either. He took a deep breath. 'Come on, then.'

He skirted the central clearing of the village, now a muddy pool, until he found the track that led away from the village, the direction Harlow had taken last night after the ceremony. He'd said he knew something about Felicity's death; it was about time Walker found out what it was.

He slowed on the muddy track. Harlow was a murderer. What could he know about Felicity? And why would he tell him? Walker had a bad feeling about the whole thing. But this was why he'd come to New Guinea, back to where it had happened. Back to where he'd lost his wife. Where Alf Runsack was probably murdered. Where he himself had almost drowned. Where he – maybe – had eaten his wife's flesh so he could survive. Now here, – in the jungle of PNG, close to where it had all happened, – he paused. He stood in the rain and closed his eyes.

It was on a day like this they had travelled north from here – he, Felicity and their guide. They'd said goodbye to Alf Runsack. He said he'd finished his report; there was no oil down here and it would be useless for any company to invest in the area. Walker hadn't thought anything about it at the time. Oil had nothing to do with why he and Felicity were there. But Alf had been adamant. Nervous too. Said he'd sent his report on before him for 'safety'. At the time, Walker hadn't known what he meant.

But later that day, none of that mattered. They were caught in the flood in the river. But before … before they were washed away in the deluge, there was something else. They were being chased. Their guide – Walker still couldn't remember his name! – was scared. He was rushing them forward, looking back as if they were being followed. And Felicity, she was scared too. Why? Did she understand more than he did? She'd talked to Alf as well. Come to think of it, she'd spent a long time talking to Alf. And she was frightened. What had Alf said to her?

Walker realised he'd stopped on the track. He became aware of the thick jungle around him on all sides. He could smell the composting, moist jungle loam, could hear the slap of the raindrops on the wide leaves, but otherwise it was silent. Even the animals had sought shelter. Why hadn't he? It was a day like the day Flea had died. He closed his eyes. He could see them now. The men following them. They had weapons – spears and machetes. Chasing them.

'Interesting place to stop.'

The voice was close to his ear and Walker jumped. He wiped the rain from his eyes.

It was Harlow standing before him in the mud, still dressed for his initiation – painted skin, grass skirt, naked chest, bulging muscles, bone through his nose. He was smiling but the red paint around his lips made him look grotesque, like a monster from a Venetian Mardi Gras.

Walker said nothing. He looked beyond Harlow and then turned behind – no one.

'Out for a walk?' asked Harlow.

'Looking for breakfast,' Walker said carefully.

Again, there was the ghastly grin. 'Hungry, are we?' A tongue came out and slithered around. 'Me too.' He pointed away from the village. 'This way. I'll go with you.'

Walker set off but then remembered the ceremony of the night before and stopped. 'Your feet. Are they okay? Were they burnt?'

'Never better. The Weyamen have all sorts of salves.' He looked down. 'They're still sore but, as you can see, I can walk.' He looked up and grinned. 'Run even, if need be.'

Walker didn't like the sound of the last. 'How did you come to be initiated into the tribe? You must have spent a lot of time with them.'

Harlow paused, as if considering his answer. 'Trust,' he said finally. 'It is hard to find men you can trust, truly believe in.   They have done a lot for me, proven themselves. So, I have faith in them. And they trust me. More than you can trust your own family. The initiation was the last sign. I trusted them when they laid those coals out for me. And I trusted in myself. Trusted that I could do it.'

Walker began walking along the trail. Harlow's answer didn't seem to explain anything. There was nothing ahead but the muddy track and thick jungle.

He stopped again and faced him. 'My wife died down here some years ago. You said you knew something about her.'

Harlow twisted the thick clown-lips, as if he was thinking. 'Your wife's death. Yes, there was something about that you probably should know.'

'What?'

'I heard that she didn't drown, as people say.'

Walker froze. 'What do you know of it?'

He waved his hand. 'Later. There's time for that sort of talk later.'

'Tell me,' demanded Walker.

'Come, I insist.' He waved again. 'I'm famished. Keep moving and we can talk while we eat.'

Reluctantly, Walker turned and continued along the trail. They came to a clearing where the track skirted the bottom of a muddy cliff-face. Water poured over the rutted cliff edge above, then spread out like a shallow stream over the surface. It was boggy.

Walker turned and faced Harlow. 'I want to know.'

Harlow gave a lurid smile. 'Tell me, there was a fellow down here at the same time as you. A geologist.'

'Alf Runsack.'

Harlow clicked his fingers. 'Runsack, yes, that's it.'

'What about him?'

'There's a story going around that he did a report.'

'What of it?'

Harlow stepped towards him, his smile gone. 'There's a story that he gave you a copy.'

Walker frowned. Then he laughed. 'Is that what this is all about? You think I've got a report about oil?'

'Do you?'

'I couldn't give a stuff about oil. Why would he give me a copy?' Harlow was watching him closely. 'And if he did, why would I still have it?'

'Maybe you didn't know the significance of it? Maybe you just thought it was a boring old report that you put somewhere?'

Walker laughed again. 'This is bloody ridiculous. You think I'd care two hoots about a few scraps of paper when I'd almost died? When my wife *had* died?' He shook his head in disbelief. 'I've come down here to find out why, and all you've got are stories about useless oil reports. You know what? I don't give a fuck! And I don't have – and have never had – Alf's stupid report.' He turned away.

He heard Harlow laugh, – deep and throaty. He was following him. 'That's funny,' Walker heard him say. He sensed Harlow had stopped again and he turned.

Harlow was leaning forward, hands on knees, giggling now.

'What's so funny?'

'You.' Harlow giggled again. 'And your friends. They've set you up.'

'I don't know what you mean.'

'They started a story to say that you had a copy of the original report. I didn't really believe them. But since you were here it was easy enough to find out. I was coming anyway.'

'So what are you going to do, kill me?'

There was no answer. The silence was ominous. All he could hear was the torrential rain smashing against the underbrush and rocks. If anything, it had picked up. Salty water streamed down his face across his lips and over his body.

Finally, Harlow did speak. 'I should've finished you the first time – just like your wife!'

'What? What are you saying?' He stepped back. 'Are you saying you killed Flea?'

'Flea!' Harlow let out a boisterous laugh, his red mouth stretched like a maniac. 'Was that her name? Oh my god!' He laughed again and slapped his thigh. 'That fits perfectly. Yes! She was nothing but an insignificant little insect. And I squashed her like a flea. Cracked her head open.'

'But she drowned –'

'No, she didn't, you fool. Is that what you thought all this time? Did *you* drown? Why should she?' Harlow watched him carefully as he edged closer. 'She washed up onto the river's edge. It was easy to finish her off. And her guide as well. I only wish I'd spent the time to look for you. You I thought *had* drowned. Sloppy of me. But I can fix that now.'

Walker felt an overwhelming rage. He cried out as he launched himself and crashed into the other man. But Harlow was ready for him and sidestepped, punching him in the side of the head as he stumbled past. Walker's head buzzed. The ground began to shake then the soil beneath his feet gave way. Now he was falling, slipping. Everything was black. He couldn't breathe. His body jerked to a halt. He couldn't move, his legs and arms were pinned down.

His head still buzzed. What had happened? Slowly, he realised …

A landslide!

He sucked in a breath and his mouth filled with mud. He coughed to clear it. He could move his left arm and he pushed the muck away from his face. There was light. So, he wasn't buried deep. There was a chance he could get out. The rain still bucketed down. All around was churned wet earth and debris. His right arm was stuck under him, useless, but he could move his left leg a little. If he could only clear a bit more mud …

A figure appeared before him on hands and knees, a glint of metal.

'Bad luck, Walker.' It was Harlow. 'Call it fate. It could've been me caught in the mud, helpless. But it's not. It's you. I'll make it fast.'

Harlow's face was close to his. Walker threw a punch with his free arm but the South African slapped it away then pinned his shoulder down. Walker felt metal on his neck. Hot fluid gushed onto his face, blinding him. His mouth filled with blood. Harlow's body pushed against his, taking his breath away, crushing him as blood washed over his face, filling his nose. Everything started to go black.

Abruptly the weight lifted, allowing Walker to take a gasping breath. He raised a hand to his eyes and tried to wipe them clear but only managed to smear muck onto them. He blinked through the grit. A black face stared down at him. A woman's. The one from the Coffee Institute. Over her shoulder was another face, a man he recognised.

'Wendy?'

'I told you to leave Harlow to us,' said the black girl over her shoulder to Darling.

Someone else was at his side digging with her hands to free his body, and Walker twisted his head. The blonde girl.

'You too? Where did you all come from?'

Within moments they had pulled him free, and Walker sat up and leaned forward, hugging his knees. Kronig's body lay on its side nearby, a long spear protruding from the neck.

'You're right about being a deadly shot with a spear, Grace,' Darling said to the dark woman.

Walker's doctor instincts kicked in and he crawled to the body and felt for the carotid pulse.

'He's dead,' Grace said flatly. 'Just like my grandpa, I never miss.'

CHAPTER THIRTY

AIR, FRESH AND sweet in his throat. No sense of sweat or humidity or blood. No mud or dirt.

Walker cracked his eyes open – sunlight through glass, the shadow of leaves swaying in a breeze.

He'd slept well.

Rested.

At last.

He took a deep breath, all the way in through his nose, all the way out through his mouth. Nothing ached, no sharp jabs of pain.

And there were no lingering memories or dreams. No nightmares.

He thought about Felicity but now in a detached sort of way. Not dismissive. He didn't feel the need to suppress her memory. He was at peace. For once, she'd not come to him in his sleep. She'd not pushed him away but neither had she come to speak to him. She was gone. Really gone. Gone to rest. Perhaps they could now be at peace with each other.

He rolled over and sat on the edge of the bed, glancing back as he did. The other side of the bed was unruffled and the pillow straight and flat. Near the door was the red, straight-backed chair – Felicity's chair. He stared at it for some moments, wondering what he should do with it. Should he get rid of it?

No, he would keep it. Felicity deserved at least that much from him. He'd be able to remember her now with fondness, not dread. He had loved her – still loved her. His memory of her.

His first love.

He stood and rubbed his hand over his bare belly. Could he love again? Could someone ever love him?

He blew out a deep breath. Right now, he really didn't care.

It was over a week since he'd got back from New Guinea and he felt as if he'd finally healed, in more ways than one. He'd locked himself up in his terrace on Lower Fort Street and not spoken a word to anyone. He didn't want to think about Barry Darling or Angela Chee or Cassandra Hollows. He didn't want to think about any of them. Slowly, slowly, the muck and guilt had gone. The blackness and badness had been leached from his mind. For the first time since Felicity's death, he felt calm. For the first time, he could think about her without the great Black welling up in his chest, covering his nose and mouth, strangling him, overpowering him. He could remember the feeling but now it did not engulf him, as if he could examine it from afar. He hoped the relief would last.

He opened the French doors and stepped out onto the veranda. A magpie warbled on a branch and a pair of noisy mynas fluttered above, squawking and diving at it. The air was warm and the sky clear. It would be a good beach day. He should go for a bodysurf.

He leaned over the bannister and looked up the street. At the top was the yellow stone of the Garrison Church, resplendent in the morning sun. Felicity and he had got married there. Maybe he should go back. Maybe now he *could* go back?

'Maybe not,' he mumbled to himself. 'Anyway, today is Saturday.'

He threw on a shirt and shorts and jogged down the stairs into the kitchen and put the kettle on. While he waited for it to boil he flicked through the stack of mail that sat on the table – mostly bills and supermarket brochures.

While studying a brochure, he poured a cup of tea and opened the back door. Archie walked in immediately, as if he'd been expecting the door to open at that precise moment. Walker bent over and scratched him under the chin and the cat arched his back against his legs. He picked him up and cradled him like a baby as he scratched his belly, triggering a deep rumble. The cat had obviously recovered from his previous incarceration with Walker.

He joggled him up and down. 'You weigh a ton, Archie. What's Janet been feeding you?'

The cat decided he'd had enough and jumped from his arms then strolled out the door into the backyard, and Walker raised his eyes to follow his path.

A mountain of a man stood there – leather jacket, tattooed neck.

'Ali,' Walker said calmly, briefly wondering why he was not more startled.

He nodded his head solemnly in greeting. 'Dr Walker. I see you've survived your overseas adventure.'

'Looks like it.' He waited for a moment but when Ali remained silent, he asked. 'What can I do for you?'

He shrugged his shoulders. 'Nothing. I was passing and thought I'd drop in.'

Walker bowed his head solemnly. 'Nice of you to call.' He pointed to the back gate, which stood ajar. 'I was just going out for breakfast. Care to join me?'

'Certainly.'

'How about the G'day Cafe?'

'Ah, one of my cousins owns that. Good choice.'

Walker suspected that Ali's use of the term 'cousin' meant that the family probably knew of each other, at best, or maybe just came from the same mountain region of Lebanon.

Twenty minutes later they were seated in the back courtyard of the cafe adjacent to the Orient Hotel, each with a plate of bacon and eggs before them.

'Are you sure you're okay eating ham?' asked Walker.

Ali stuffed a loaded fork into his mouth. 'My cousin is very skilful,' he said with a wink as he swallowed. 'And discreet. If anyone asks, this is halal.'

Walker ate his own food in silence, knowing Ali would eventually come to the purpose of his visit. He thought maybe he just wanted to make sure he'd not spoken to the cops about his possible involvement with the heroin affair, which had led to the murders two months ago.

When he'd finally wiped his plate clean and finished his last sip of cappuccino, Ali leaned back in his seat with a satisfied look.

'Dr Walker,' he began, 'I wanted to ask you a favour.'

Here it comes. 'What?' said Walker.

Ali picked up a toothpick and began digging it into his gums. 'I have a fancy to find out about Christianity.'

That was not what he'd expected. He examined the large Muslim carefully for any evidence of jest. 'A fancy?'

'An interest,' he said seriously. 'No. More than that. A yearning.'

'A yearning.'

'Yes.' Ali gave an emphatic nod. 'Yes, I think I'd describe it as a yearning.'

'You're pulling my leg.'

He raised his hands defensively. 'Not at all. I'm serious.'

Walker placed his fingers on his own chest. 'But why would you ask me?'

'You're the only Christian I know.'

'I would hardly call myself a Christian.'

'Well, you are more of a Christian than I am.'

'That's not very hard.' He frowned and examined Ali again. 'Why do you want to find out about Christianity?'

Ali leaned back in his chair and nodded slowly, as if Walker had finally accepted his supposition and was now testing him. 'Because this is a Christian land. And if I want to get ahead, I think I should become a Christian.'

Walker's frown deepened. He tapped the tabletop in thought. 'Really?'

'Really.'

He felt relieved. If all the big Leb wanted to do was become a Christian then it was fine by him. Better than any other unsavoury favour he could've asked for.

'Well,' he said slowly, 'I guess I could introduce you to the rector up at the Garrison Church. Can't do any harm.'

Ali sat forward. 'That would be much appreciated. Do you know him well?'

'No, not really. Or not at all, actually. I used to go to church there when I was a kid but the rector has probably changed.' He scratched his head. 'But I've been thinking about going back to church on Sunday. Maybe we can go together.'

Ali stood up and clapped his hands. 'Perfect. That is what I hoped you'd say. I've already cased the joint this morning. They have a service tomorrow at ten. I'll come to your place at nine thirty?'

Before he could say anything, Ali was gone, swaggering out through the front door of the cafe after throwing a few bills down on the counter with a wave to his cousin.

Walker watched him go with a feeling of incredulity. 'Blimey,' he murmured to himself, 'going back to church. And with a Lebanese Muslim of all things!'

Barry Darling caught up with Sally Briggs two hours after he'd landed at Kingsford Smith Airport from Port Moresby, taking a taxi straight to his house, throwing his bags down then immediately leaving to meet her. They came together on the footpath outside the Glebe cafe and Sally initially stood away from him, unsmiling, examining his face closely as if looking for clues. Then abruptly, she lunged forward and hugged him tightly. He hugged her back, worried he might squash the air out of her, such was his verve, but she buried her face in his shoulder and squeezed back just as hard.

'I was worried you might not come back,' she whispered when he'd finally loosened his grip. 'Worried you might have been hurt.'

'No chance of that,' he said. 'I had too many people looking after me.'

'People?' She had a worried look. 'I heard the news. A man killed in the highlands. Speared. I thought it was you.'

'No, not me. But I can't say much about that right now. Still before the courts. I have to race off and report to Superintendent Bowles at The Rocks Station. But I wanted to talk to you first. I need to tell you something.' He pointed to a table outside the cafe. 'Cappuccino?' His face was grim.

'What do you need to tell me?' she asked after the coffees were served.

Darling hesitated, head down, playing with the foam on the top of the coffee with his spoon.

Sally looked distressed. 'Is there something wrong?' When he remained silent, she reared back in her seat. 'What are you going to tell me? It's bad, I can tell.' She looked like she was going to break into tears.

'Not so much tell you,' Darling said finally, 'but ask you. I'm just not sure …'

'Ask me?' she said uncertainly. 'Not sure about what?'

'Not sure whether you'll agree.'

'Agree to what?'

'I got the house. The one on Bridge Street. The two-bedder.' He reached his hand across the table towards hers. 'I was going to ask you … whether you want to move in with me.'

She screamed, then stifled the sound by placing her hands over her mouth. Her face exploded with joy and she giggled. Then she grabbed his hand, her face still lit up like a child's at a Christmas fair. 'Yes!' She laughed aloud. 'The answer is yes.'

Barry Darling found Superintendent Fred Bowles in his office at the rear of The Rocks Police Station a short time later. The stout policeman sat hunched over his desk studying a report, his finger tracing the line he was reading, his neck creased, accentuating his generous jowls. When Bowles caught sight of Darling, he scooped the folder up and waved it at him.

'Makes nice reading, Wendy. Got the bastard in the neck, eh? Just like he deserved.'

'Well, not me, sir. It was an ASIS agent. Saved Kit's life.'

'How did the spooks get tangled up in it? It was a good job they were? What was the name of the agent who saved Kit?'

'Grace Grimes. She was the Aboriginal girl from the Holiday Inn. She and her partner, Emma Spicer, had been tailing Harlow.'

Bowles ran a sweaty hand over his jaw. 'You don't say. An Aboriginal?'

'Torres Strait Islander, actually. From Mer. That's where Eddie Mabo comes from.'

Bowles gave a look as if Darling was speaking a foreign language. Darling continued. 'Used to be head-hunters. Her grandfather was, at least. But she's an expert shot with the spear. Got Harlow straight through the artery in his neck from ten metres to stop him skewering Kit with a knife.'

'Really,' said Bowles. 'Did you find out what the difference is?'

Darling was confused. 'Between what?'

'Aboriginals and Torres Strait Islanders?'

Darling looked deflated. 'Not really.' He shrugged. 'Didn't think to ask.'

Bowles pulled his mouth down, as if Darling had confessed an embarrassing weakness. 'Not to worry.'

'It was all about oil,' said Darling. 'Or at least the promise of oil.' He told him the story of Runsack's report and the fake one that replaced it, and how it was used to entice the big oil corporations to build roads into the area. 'A PNG public servant was in on it. Getting kickbacks, of course. Pleaded that he was just trying to help the country when he was finally arrested. My partner in PNG, Peter Token, steered the investigation that led to the arrest. Good man, Pete. He's going to go far in the AFP.'

'Wouldn't like to be in that public servant's shoes,' said Bowles.

Darling grimaced. 'I'm not sure. I don't hold any faith in the system of that country.'

'Well, it has nothing to do with us now. Our murderer's dead and the other suspects have ended up being bloody Australian intelligence agents.' He wiped his hands together. 'Nothing more for us to do.'

'Guess so.' His official report over, Darling took a seat opposite the senior officer with a pensive look.

'What?' said Bowles. 'Out with it.'

'It's about Felicity. Turns out she was murdered. By Harlow. He also murdered the guide.'

'So she didn't drown?'

'No. Maybe also explains the crack in the skull.'

'You don't look convinced.'

Darling's face gave nothing away. 'I saw them. They looked like holes, not cracks.'

'What are you saying?'

'The local coppers from Mount Hagen – the ones who took me to the shack – they thought it looked like funerary rites.'

'Funeral rites?'

'Funerary – a ceremony to do with dead relatives.' Darling paused before continuing. 'In that part of the world they used to eat the corpses. The brains.'

Bowles shifted his considerable bulk in his chair and scowled. 'So, you're saying that Felicity had her skull drilled open after she was dead so someone could eat her brains.'

'I'm not saying that,' Darling said quickly.

'Sounds to me like you are,' growled Bowles. He raised a finger. 'I'm gonna have to warn you again, Wendy. Be very, very careful about bandying around unfounded rumours. Kit has come through a lot. He doesn't need that sort of shit piled on him.'

He nodded solemnly. 'I know, I know. I agree. I think I'll have to let that one rest. At least I'm sure Kit had nothing to do with desecrating Felicity's body. He was completely out of it.' He sat silently for some moments. 'Gotta leave it. Gotta leave it,' he mumbled, shaking his head.

'Anything else?' Bowles asked. 'How's your spontaneous combustion case going?'

Darling noticed Bowles was now wearing an indulgent smirk. 'Haven't heard,' he said, rising to his feet. He took a deep breath then stuck out his hand. 'Good to see you again, Fred. Thanks for everything you've done, now and in the past. Probably won't be back, so I thought I'd better say it.'

The large man took his hand and shook it then watched grimly as Darling walked away.

CHAPTER THIRTY-ONE

ALI AND WALKER entered the Garrison Church at fifteen minutes before ten on the Sunday. It was a beautiful autumn day, twenty-eight degrees with clear blue skies but inside the church it was dark and gloomy. Someone was playing an organ near the front. No one greeted them at the door but already there were people scattered among the pews waiting for the service to begin. Walker found a spot halfway up on the left, behind a large pillar.

His eyes slowly adjusted to the light and he looked around at the stained-glass windows and the plaques that decorated the walls, which commemorated those lost in past wars. Across the aisle on the right-hand side, he was surprised to see the rotund form of Bruce Rowntree, dressed as usual in his crumpled suit, sitting next to the white-haired Shirley, the president of the Rocks Action Group. Shirley's presence he could understand but Rowntree's shonky pastimes did not sit well with the thought of him being a Christian. *Takes all sorts, I suppose.* He remembered reading somewhere that the biggest sinners were Christians since they needed forgiveness more than others. It made him feel a bit better being there.

The service started with a hymn, which the congregation sang with gusto, sometimes drowning out the organ. It was about a fount and blessings and sonnets, which sounded more like a country and western tune than a hymn, and Walker and Ali self-consciously mumbled some of the words. There were prayers and then another hymn and then a sermon. The minister was an older man, balding at the front with high hair at the back, and dressed in a simple white smock and collar over black trousers. Walker was surprised to recognise him as the same minister who had married Felicity and him nearly a decade ago. For some reason, he'd thought that ministers would circulate to other churches.

Walker settled himself down to be bored for the next twenty minutes and figured that after Ali had sat through the same mundane sermon, he'd change his mind about wanting to become a Christian. He had doubts about how serious Ali was and suspected the bikie had an ulterior motive.

But the sermon soon captured Walker's attention.

'Is this life all we have?' asked the minister from the pulpit. 'Is this it? Is this as good as it gets? Do we struggle through our short miserable lives, having a few good times here and there, ultimately being left to decompose in the dirt to become recycled by worms?'

Walker sat up straight. He'd often asked himself the same question.

'Well, the answer is …' The minister paused for effect. 'Yes.'

What!? thought Walker. That didn't seem right.

'Our lives are but a fleeting moment. A wisp of air. Less than that!' The minister swung his head around at the congregation, who all looked back intently. 'In the scheme of the universe … fourteen billion years …' His voice boomed around the church, 'our lives are inconsequential fragments … fluff that gets blown away by the next wind. Vapour. Less than a puff of smoke. Meaningless.'

Walker squirmed in his seat and frowned sideways at Ali, who had his eyes glued forward, his mouth open in anticipation. This was not what Walker had been expecting.

'And I bet you all think that you're all hot stuff. I reckon there'd be a couple of lawyers here, maybe a few doctors and other professionals, elder statesmen who have put their lives into the community, businessmen and women who have built little empires. And you've done it all yourself, haven't you? You've put in the hard yards. Through hard work, intelligence, clever strategy and luck, you've got where you are – some better than others, but all of us pretty comfortable compared to the rest of the world.

'Well, you know what?' The minister looked around at his audience again. 'That's all just bull-twang!'

Walker's frown deepened. He couldn't remember sermons being like this.

The minister raised his finger and pointed. Walker thought he might be pointing at him. 'You've all done nothing, except to have been born and managed to exist. Know this. No clever deed you've done actually comes from you. You might be intelligent, you might be good-looking, you might have worked like a dog to get where you are. You can look at yourself smugly and pat yourself on the back and tell yourself that you've done a job well. You deserve what you've got. *You* have done it. The unique thing inside *you* has allowed you to rise to the top. Bull-twang!

'Let me tell you, it's *not* you. No! All of it, every last bit, comes from our Lord God. He has given it to you. It's not from you at all.'

More than one person looked sideways at their neighbour. Feet shuffled and here and there, people murmured.

'You come here. I'm sure you all have your reasons. But are you true? Do you believe?'

Walker looked down at his pamphlet in case the minister caught his eye.

'It is a *fact*,' he shouted the word, 'that a man we call Jesus Christ was crucified by the Romans two thousand years ago. That is an historical fact. No one contradicts it. Just as factual as the holocaust or World War One or the existence of the Roman Empire.

'It is also *fact* that that same man rose from the dead three days later. Witnesses saw him. Almost a hundred witnesses. That is also fact.' He stared out at the congregation and his voice dropped. 'It is also a miracle.' He smiled and nodded his head knowingly. 'But we don't believe in miracles these days, do we? We're all too clever for that. Too scientific. Too logical.' His lip curled up in disgust.

'And the other thing we are asked to believe is that that man was also God.' He stood upright, both hands on the pulpit. 'But there's the twist.' He hunched his shoulders and tapped his skull. 'We are all so smart, aren't we? Educated. We can explain so many things – the atom, gravity, the Big Bang. We can send a man to the moon. We can prove anything we wish to be either true or false. We have conquered the world and nature. We can even end our own world if we wish.

'But it is all vapour. Nothing!' He pointed. 'You. Will. All. Die. Your carcasses will rot in the dirt, some sooner, some later. But it will happen to every one of us, me included.

'We strive. We work, we cajole others to do what we want. We do good things. We do bad things, horrific things. We're nasty to the ones we love and nice to those who are nasty to us. I include myself in all of this. We're all the same.

'So today, I am going to give you one piece of advice, if you care to take it.' He paused and looked around the dim room. 'Give it up. Stop believing that you're God's gift to mankind. We're *all* His gift, not just you. Bad people just as much as your good *special* self. And stop believing that your achievements come from you. That is our biggest sin. Thinking we can do it all on our own. Because you know what? If you believe that then all your failures – all your weaknesses, all your disappointment – they're *your* fault too, not someone else's. And we all fail. Every day. Stop believing that you determine your own destiny. Instead, believe in our God who loves you. He is your destiny.

'And you need to fear him. He is not a nice, sugar-coated Father Christmas that we can keep in the closet and pull out when it's convenient. If that's what you do, you'll rot in hell for eternity. You can be good. You can have Christian values. You can be nice to people, care about them. But if you ignore your God – if you treat him like a nice old uncle that gives you lollies if you're good – then you've been wasting your time. No, you need to fear him! He can tear you to pieces in a moment, take away everything you have in a second. But he does love you. He will support you, give you what you need, even if you don't know it.'

The minister closed his eyes. 'Then, and only then, our miserable lives mean something. *Something*, not nothing. Our short lives are not puffs of smoke, ready to be blown away by an uncaring universe. After the worms eat our flesh and our friends and family have forgotten what we even used to look like, and the world has forgotten about all our marvellous deeds, we *will* be somewhere. We will be with our God for eternity.'

He opened his eyes and smiled. 'And yes, it's that simple. All you have to do is believe and ask for His grace and you will have it. That's the thing a lot of people don't understand. All you have to do is ask for it.' He shook his head. 'It's not a trick. In this one thing, what sounds too good to be true is *actually* true.'

He stepped back from the edge of his pulpit and dropped his head. 'That is all I have to say today. Sometimes I feel I must stop beating around the bush. What you have to do is simple. Believe in Jesus Christ. Stop thinking that it's *you* who determines your destiny. Ask for God's grace. Then, and only then, your life will have meaning.

'"Trust in the Lord with all your heart

'And lean not on your own understanding;

'In all your ways submit to him,

'And he will make your paths straight".'

The minister said a short prayer then the organ started again and people sang but Walker couldn't get the words from his mind. The service finally ended and people began to file out.

Walker turned to Ali. 'What did you think?'

'After that, I definitely want to become a Christian.' Ali looked genuine.

'Okay, let's meet the minister then. He might even remember me.'

As they moved along the pew, a figure became visible who had been sitting in front of them but had been obscured by the column.

Walker stopped. 'Angela!'

She twisted in the seat. 'Chris! What are you doing here?'

'I live down the road. This is my church.'

'I didn't think you went to church?'

'I'm thinking of coming back.' He turned to his friend. 'This is Ali. He's thinking of becoming a Christian.'

Angela nodded to Ali but seemed reticent to talk.

'What did you think of the sermon?' Walker asked.

'I found it made sense for my life.'

Walker hesitated. 'Ali, can I have a word with Angela? I can catch up with you outside, if you like.'

After Ali left, Walker sat down beside Angela in the pew.

'How was New Guinea?' she asked.

'I found out how Felicity died. She was murdered. Her killer is dead. To tell the truth, I feel relieved.' He rubbed his neck. 'I had a horrible feeling that I'd somehow killed her, or at least let her die.'

She reached out and took his hand. 'That all sounds so terrible. Are you okay?' When he gave an indefinite shrug, she squeezed his hand. 'You'll have to tell me the whole story one day.' She looked around to make sure they were alone. 'Chris, I'm sorry about everything before. About me being … distant. I'm better now.' She looked towards the main door of the church where the minister was greeting the congregation. Most had gone. The large form of Ali Harb was silhouetted in the doorway, talking to him. Angela nodded towards the minister. 'He's been helping me. The psychologists you met, they referred me to him. I'm beginning to believe that I'm normal. That I'm not like my mother.'

It was his turn to squeeze her hand. 'That's good. I'm happy for you. If it means anything, I never thought you were. For that matter, I was never sure your mother was like that either.'

Angela looked around at the empty pews, as if she wanted to talk of something else. She turned back. 'I hear you're seeing Cassie.'

Walker shook his head. 'No. I was. Not now …'

She waited.

He sat back in the pew. 'After what happened … finding out the truth about Felicity … things are different.' He looked at her. 'I'm different. I feel like a heavy weight has been lifted off me. Like I can breathe again.'

She leaned towards him. 'Does Cassie know how you feel?'

'No. I haven't seen her.'

'You're going to have to see her sometime.'

Walker shrugged. 'Sure. Not now. Later.'

She smiled meekly. 'We could spend some time together, if you like.' Then she appeared as if she thought she'd been too forward. 'If you would like to, that is.'

'Of course I would.' He looked back towards the door. Ali and the minister were still deep in conversation. 'What about tonight?

'Oh.' She made a nondescript face. 'I guess so.'

'What about the Thai restaurant near your place? Nothing too complicated.'

'Sounds nice. Nothing too complicated.' Then she smiled. 'Sure, I'd love to come.'

CHAPTER THIRTY-TWO

WALKER GOT TO the clinic at Western Meadows Hospital early on the Monday morning. He'd been gone for weeks and somehow he had to make it up to those who had covered him, most of all Angela.

Angela and he had spent an awkward evening at a Thai restaurant on the main drag at Epping. She seemed to be distracted and their conversation stilted. At the end of the evening, he'd courteously walked her back to her flat, then left after a brief hug. 'Nothing too complicated,' he'd muttered, as he drove away.

For once, he was the first doctor in the clinic, arriving shortly after 8 am. The nurses were there, of course.

There was a general stir as he entered, like a dog turning up to a meerkat convention – heads raised, faces together for short conversations, then scurrying away to other duties as if there was nothing going on out of the ordinary. Eventually, one of the Filipino nurses sauntered up to him.

'You're back, Dr Walker,' she said, as if the bleeding obvious needed to be stated. 'You've been away for three weeks and now you're back. Early. You never come to the clinic early.' Her lips curled into a smile but her eyes didn't match it. 'What's *wrong* with you?'

Walker let out a laugh, carefree and true. 'Nothing. Nothing at all.' He beamed with delight. 'Just thought I should be on time, for a change.'

The nurse shook her head. 'Something is wrong,' she grumped as she turned away.

Angela turned up ten minutes later looking fresh and elegant, which was the signal for the nurses to congregate in the clinic room and watch the interaction between the two doctors.

'Good morning, Dr Walker,' Angela said warmly, glancing briefly at the semicircle of clinic staff.

The nurses appeared dissatisfied with the exchange.

'Thought I'd better pull my weight for a change,' said Walker, gesturing to the stack of patient files that sat on the counter.

Angela's eyes followed his hand. 'I've asked a few patients to come back. I wasn't sure what to do.'

'No problem.'

She rifled through the stack and pulled out a file. 'Mrs Boyce, for one. She's had her surgery.' Angela glanced up from the file with a slight smile. 'Kidney cancer metastasis to the duodenum, as predicted. All resected, margins clear.'

The nurses gave each other unsatisfied looks then drifted away.

Walker put his head to the side, trying his hardest not to look pleased. Betty Boyce had been investigated for anaemia for months without a diagnosis until Walker had insisted on the resection. The surgeons had been dubious. 'Is she okay?'

'Surprisingly well. Her follow-up CT shows no other metastases. She's back to her normal weight. Thinking of going back to work. Do you think she needs any other treatment?'

'Nope. You never know, the cancer might not come back. Sometimes those with solitary metastases are cured by the resection.'

Angela raised her eyebrows. 'Weird. Why do you think?'

'Must have something to do with the immune system killing the other microscopic deposits. Or at least preventing them from taking hold. You know, there's a spontaneous remission rate for renal cell cancer.' He reached out his hand for the file. 'I'll see her, if you like.'

After Betty Boyce had left, Angela poked her head into his clinic room. 'Sandra Wright wants to say hello.'

When Walker gave a puzzled look, Angela came all the way in and closed the door. 'The lady with the metastatic breast cancer.' When he was still blank-faced she added, 'Pericardial effusion? Tamponade? Almost died on the ward? Had to stick a twelve-inch needle into her heart?'

'Oh yes,' he said finally, recalling. 'Susan Wright, of course. I remember.'

'Sandra. *Sandra* Wright.'

'Yes, Sandra Wright. I said I remember her.'

Sandra was bald but was wearing makeup and appeared healthy. 'You seem really well, Sandra,' said Walker.

'Fourth cycle next week,' she said. 'And Dr Chee says that we can stop after that.' She gave Walker a pleading look.

Walker flicked through the notes. 'Of course. Your cancer is hormone receptor positive. You can start tamoxifen, which should keep the cancer under control for a long time. It's a hormone tablet. An oestrogen blocker.'

'How long?' she asked pointedly. 'How long will it keep the cancer under control?'

'For years in some women.' Sandra seemed content with the answer and did not press him further. 'It would be good to see you get back to your normal life as soon as the chemo is finished. How about we see you in another month and talk about the tamoxifen then.'

Soon the clinic area was empty. Even the nurses had gone to lunch, leaving Walker and Angela by themselves.

Walker turned to her. 'Where does that leave us, Angela? I've been thinking about it a lot. I want to know if we have a future.'

She bent her head, causing her dark fringe to hide her eyes. 'Not sure, Chris. A lot has happened in the last few months, to us and around us.' She looked up, her soft brown eyes locked onto his. 'But I have to tell you something. I wanted to tell you last night but couldn't.'

His breath stopped in his throat. He didn't like how she'd said that. He remained silent, unable to answer.

'I've got another job.' She waited for him to speak and when he didn't, she continued. 'I can't keep working here. My father's death, my arrest for his murder. Everyone looks at me when I walk past as if they think I killed him, despite everything. They know about the metoprolol.' She closed her eyes and leaned against the wall and blew out a large breath. 'And then there's you and me. I've acted like a total fruitcake. No matter what you say, you'll always know what I was like. I don't want to go into a relationship like that.'

She opened her eyes and looked at him again. Walker was frozen, unable to speak, unable to think.

'And then there's Cassie. You haven't even said anything to her about us. That says something to me about how serious you are.'

Finally, he was able to utter something. 'But this is not supposed to happen. Everything is sorted. Felicity, me, you. Even Wendy and I are speaking. Everything is how it's supposed to be.'

She looked at him carefully, as if he was fragile. 'Maybe it is as you say. But you and I aren't right. We can't be together. Not now.' She paused, then added gently, 'Maybe not ever.'

'But where will you go?'

'Singapore. I've got a job at the National Cancer Institute. And it turns out my family there *do* want to see me, after all. I have an aunty. She's like my mother. I want to spend time with her. I want to get to know my family.'

Walker let out a shaky breath. Hesitantly, he nodded. 'I can see that. I can see you want to get to know your family.' He didn't want to think about the other parts – the parts about him. 'When will you go?'

'Tomorrow. My flight's booked. One-way.'

He wondered why she felt obliged to say the last, as if to rub in how much she didn't want to come back to him. He was about to say that maybe he'd visit her, but he stopped himself. He wasn't sure he wanted to. And he was very sure she wouldn't want him to either.

He realised he had nothing else to say. He turned away and began to walk along the corridor. At the end, he stopped and turned back. 'Good luck,' he called, then turned away, not waiting for a response.

He walked out of the clinic towards the main entrance of the hospital and then out into the sunshine. It was a beautiful autumn day, warm without being too hot, with a light breeze blowing. The sky was an unbroken blue and birds flitted and twittered above, chasing each other playfully.

He felt numb. Apprehensive. Heartbroken? But he was surprised. It wasn't like the Black. He was sad but he could still feel. There was no hole in his chest threatening to pull him in. He concentrated, forcing himself to go deep down to where that awfulness had lived. To the Black. But it wasn't there. It had gone. Gone like Felicity. She'd taken it with her.

He took a deep breath in and blew it out slowly then gazed up at the sky. He played with his lip thoughtfully.

Things could be worse.

Then he noticed the large bulk of his intern, Vince Greenway, walking towards him from the street and he waved to him.

'Nice day, Dr Walker,' Vince called as he passed.

'Certainly is,' he said.

'Great day for a body surf.'

Walker nodded to himself after the intern had gone. 'Certainly is,' he repeated softly. 'A beer at the Hero then a body surf at Tamarama it is then.' He turned to walk back into the hospital and whistled a nondescript tune.

I wonder if Cassie's free tonight?

Then he noticed Jason Shore coming out of the main door of the hospital carrying a cardboard box.

'Dr Walker,' Jason said. 'Fancy meeting you here. I'm just picking up Dad's belongings.' He nodded at a blue four-wheel drive parked in the No Standing zone nearby. 'Do you mind?'

As Walker opened the passenger door, something dropped from the car into the gutter. Before he could pick it up, Jason hoisted the box onto the front seat then stooped to retrieve the item. He stood and opened his palm. In it was a gold necklace. Walker saw the fish and the torn clasp before Jason's fist curled into a ball, which he thrust into his pocket.

Walker raised his eyes.

Jason's lips curled into a smile but his eyes were cold.

'For my father, Dr Walker.'

END OF BOOK 3

The story continues in
Murder in the Mists

Author's note

THE MAIN CHARACTERS in this novel are completely fictional. If you think you recognise yourself or someone you have worked with then you're wrong!

This might disappoint those who think this series is some sort of exposé of a Sydney teaching hospital. Of course, like any story, all characters and situations are necessarily based on memories of real people and events. But I can assure you that all main characters are the product of my imagination.

There are many historical names that are obviously real. I have never met any of these people and any mention of them in the book is a construction of events from public records.

Many of the historical details are accurate, such as contemporary news items, names of songs and television shows, and the names and position of restaurants and pubs in Sydney in 1991. Some details are inaccurate and I intentionally departed from the facts for the purposes of this fictional story.

The medical cases are descriptions of events I or my colleagues have been involved with over the years, although the patient names are fictional.

Discover other titles by Howard Gurney

Path to Chaos series (fantasy)
Twin
The Thread Frays
Chaos

Dr Christopher Walker Murder Mystery series
Murder on the Ward
Death in a Chapel
Murder at The Rocks

Thank you for reading my book. If you enjoyed it, please take a moment to leave a review at your favourite retailer.

Howard Gurney

www.howardgurney.com

@HowardGurney

www.ingramcontent.com/pod-product-compliance
Lightning Source LLC
Chambersburg PA
CBHW030423120726
47903CB00003B/785